Sherlock Holmes: The Greatest Detective

I0607852

The Hounds Of Baskerville

By Todd Black

Table of Contents

Prologue: Hunted

Night in the forest.

The wind swept across the tops of the trees, cooling the air and filling it with noise. In a small clearing deep in the forest, a man lied unconscious on the ground. He laid there for some time, until slowly he stirred. The man groaned as he rose to a kneeling position and tried to get a bearing on where he was. Before he could do that though, his body ringed with pain.

"Ow," he said to himself.

His head was pounding, as he reached towards the back of his head to try and ease the pain he recoiled. There was a lump there, something had hit him hard.

"Did I get knocked out?"

Pushing through the pain and the uncertainty of what was going on, he rose to his feet. The man looked around to try and get a clue as to where he was. He was wearing jeans and a flannel sweatshirt, wrapped around his neck was an intricate red scarf. It danced in the wind as he looked around. A thought came upon him, and he searched his pockets for the items he carried on him, his wallet was there, as was his phone. He pulled it out quickly and tried to use it, but there was no signal. With a groan he put it away and looked around again.

He got more and more worried as no clues as to exactly where he was appeared, "Ok, I'm in the forest. But is it the one next to the town? I got to figure out what's going--"

A loud rustling of leaves got his attention, he froze as he stared at a bush on one edge of the clearing, it began to rustle louder and more frequently. The man looked at the ground around him and grabbed two rocks. With haste he threw one at the bush, and from it a fox shot out that made for another side of the clearing before disappearing into the forest once more.

The main sighed in relief, then took some deep breaths to calm himself, "Yeah, smooth, almost hurt a fox. Got to get out of here. Ok, which way is south?"

He looked up to the sky, the stars were shining brightly upon him. Using his finger he mapped out constellations until he found what he was looking for.

"There! North star. North is that way, which means south is this way. Let's go."

With confidence, he stepped into the forest, he also dropped the rock he had in his other hand. But a few steps later he stopped, turned around, and picked it back up.

"Just in case."

Carefully, he made his way into the forest. He took each step with care, as he had no idea what else could be out there hidden among the trees. He used one hand to move any and all branches or obstacles that got in his way, and he kept the hand with the rock in a good position so that he could throw it at a moment's notice.

The further he went into the forest, the more he stopped to make sure he was going south. The trees were too tall to climb, so he had to search for openings through the canopies. He always seemed to find one, and kept going south because of it.

After an hour or so of walking, he took a break. The man slumped against a tree and breathed heavily, "This forest goes on forever, just glad I'm alone here."

Suddenly, a howl filled the air. It was long, and loud, and seemed to be far away. The man froze upon hearing this, and didn't move until long after the howl died down.

"Just a wolf...there are wolves in forests...just keep moving before--"

Before he could finish, another howl came, this one closer, then another, and another. These were followed by the sounds of barking that were really close. Not hesitating, the man broke into a sprint the opposite direction of the howls.

The man dare not look behind him, but instead focused all his attention to the trees and branches that now filled his path. His heart pounded as he tried to get away from what he feared was after him. This only intensified when he heard the barks return, and they were very close to where he was.

Not long after, a rustling up ahead got his attention, he didn't stop though. As soon as he went past it, a form jumped out of the bushes and roared toward him. The man dodged just in time, and the being hit a tree and fell to the ground with a whimper.

The man continued on, and the attacks became more and more frequent, only after the third time did he notice that it was a dog of some kind that was attacking him, but then the horror set in when after another attack he noticed that not only was it multiple dogs, but that their eyes were glowing.

Adrenaline getting even stronger, he tried to get away from them, but with each passing second, more and more dogs, and more and more strikes, were coming. Some were able to get in some scratches on the man, but he didn't let it deter him from trying to flee.

Eventually the man saw a clearing and sped towards it, but all relief that he had when he saw it was gone the moment he entered.

"No," he said fearfully, "no!"

What he saw in the clearing horrified him, but he could only react to it for the briefest of moments, for not long after, the dogs had caught up to him.

"Stop, no, stop!!!"

His words fell on death ears, as the dogs attacked him in unison, clawing, scratching, biting him repeatedly. The man tried to fight back, but it was no use. Soon, the dogs landed the killing blows, and the man fell limp to the ground once again. But this time, he did not get up.

The dogs circled their prey, their eyes gazing upon him, then each other. They did this for some time, until something caught their ears, they froze for a moment, ears perking upright to ensure they caught the sound, then they all rushed away.

Silence soon filled the clearing, the man's lifeless body became a stain upon the beauty that was the forest, but there it laid. Another rustling noise soon filled the air, from it came one final dog.

This one though was different, its eyes did not glow, and it stared at the man's body with something close to sympathy.

The dog approached the body, nudged it a few times, then waited. When the body did not stir, it let out a sorrowful howl.

It made to leave, but something caught its eye. The man's scarf had fallen to the ground in the attack. The dog went to it, and picked it up in its mouth. Once secured, he left the clearing, and the forest was soon quiet once more.

Chapter One: Mysteries Of the Past And Present

In London, England, at 221B Baker St., Sherlock Holmes and John Watson sat in their living room in their chairs, each of them with a newspaper in their hands. In fact, they each had the same newspaper, and were even on the same page as the other.

Both of them were looking at the page with scrutiny, as well as deep thought. Sherlock's eyes darted from the newspaper before him to Watson, who was very calm as he looked at his own paper.

"You're not going to beat me Watson," teased Sherlock with a grin.

"This time, you're wrong," replied Watson still calm.

"My record in these races is impeccable, you know that."

"I do know that, but today is different."

"How so?"

"Because you've said that you were going to beat me five times now. Usually you only do it once."

"So?"

This time Watson smiled, "That means you're stuck on something, and you're trying to get into my head so we can at least tie. I know how losing deflates your ego."

Sherlock scoffed and refocused on the paper. Before his eyes was a crossword puzzle, just about all the words were filled in, but one wasn't. It was a three letter word, with "N" being the only clue as to what it was, and it was at the end of the word.

He went through all the words it could possibly be in his head, his mouth silently saying every single one, hoping that the answer would click within his mind. Watson watched with glee as he saw Sherlock struggle, then focused back on his own puzzle.

A few minutes passed, and Sherlock was still focusing on that singular word, each moment making him more and more frustrated that the answer didn't come to him. Soon though, Watson put down his paper and looked at Sherlock, "Done."

Sherlock sprang up and pointed intently at Watson, "Lies! You cheated!"

"Oh really? How did I do that?"

He surveyed Watson, looking for any indication of foul play, but he didn't find any. His expression grew sour at this, "Fine, you didn't cheat."

"Glad we can agree on that. You seriously didn't finish?"

Sherlock growled and looked away, causing Watson to laugh.

"It's not funny Watson."

Watson fought through the laugh, "Yes it is! Like you said, you have a great record with these puzzles. We've done this for a year and a half now, and I haven't beaten you once! What one did you miss? The "Russian road brawler?"

"Zangief."

"Wow, you play that game?"

"No, one of my Undefined's does though, wouldn't shut up about him last time I used them."

"Oh, ok. Which one then?"

Sherlock rolled his eyes, "17 across."

Watson mouthed the answer, but couldn't remember which one that was, he went to the paper and look at the question pertaining to that one. Almost immediately upon looking at it he burst back into laughter, making Sherlock even more angry.

"Feel free to stop any time, Watson."

He couldn't though, and almost doubled over on the ground because of the laughing fit he was in. Watson fought hard to get back to his feet just so he could look at

Sherlock's face, "Are you seriously trying to tell me that you don't know what the Earth revolves around?"

Sherlock looked at him bitterly and shrugged, "Does it look like I watch the Earth constantly? How should I know what the Earth revolves around?"

"The sun, Sherlock! The Earth revolves around the sun!"

At this reveal, Sherlock became intrigued, even going into thought about the knowledge Watson had bestowed upon him, "Really? Fascinating. I guess that does make sense to a degree."

Watson was flabbergasted at this reply, "To a degree? That's common knowledge!"

"Clearly not, since I didn't know it."

Thinking this was the end of the chat, he picked up his paper and moved to the kitchen. Not letting him get away that easily, Watson followed, "Hold on, how did the school you went to not teach you that?"

"I didn't take an astronomy class in college Watson," noted Sherlock as he rummaged through the cupboard.

His casual response made Watson irritated, "No, not college, school! Like grade school, middle school, high school, those schools!"

"Oh, I didn't have that. I was homeschooled by my parents. My first official school was college."

A silence filled the kitchen, this got Sherlock's attention, and he slowly turned to Watson, who was once again fighting to contain a laugh. This time Sherlock got irritated, "What?"

"Nothing." answered Watson, choking on the laughs he containing.

"What!?"

"It's just... you're homeschooled... that explains a lot."

Sherlock turned to face him fully, "Homeschooling is an academically proven practice, Watson. It's known the world over, and my parents were good teachers."

"Oh I know it's a good practice, I've had friends, and a girlfriend, that were homeschooled. But..."

"But?"

"None of them turned out like you."

Watson again went into a laughing fit, and Sherlock shook his head in disgust before he went back to looking through the cupboards for things. While Watson continued to laugh, Sherlock made himself a small snack.

Eventually, Watson sobered up, "You do realize the irony in that right? I've wondered for years how you don't get along with people the way we get along. At first, I thought it was your ego, that I was the only one to put up with it. Then, I thought it was your views on intelligence--"

Sherlock stopped making his snack and whirled around, pointing at Watson with a very serious expression on his face, "I don't hate dumb people, I hate it when people do dumb things, or don't try to make themselves better after doing said dumb things."

"And I respect that...to an extent."

"Fair enough."

He went back to making his snack, but Watson just continued to stare at him as if he was a whole new person, "Still though, I never would've thought that the first true interaction that lasted with someone not family...was me. Right?"

Sherlock sighed heavily and nodded, "Right. My parents were very protective of me and Mycroft. They saw our "gifts" and were eager to bring them out to our fullest potential. So, they raised us in the knowledge they felt was useful. Astronomy wasn't one of them."

"That makes sense. Did they want you to be a detective?"

"No."

"Then what?"

"Another time, please."

He looked to Watson with honest eyes to make him stop, and Watson nodded at his request, "Of course, Sherlock. Wait, one last question, how have we not talked about this before in the twelve-ish years I've known you?"

Sherlock chuckled, "Don't you remember our agreement when we became roommates?"

"Agreement? Oh...you mean that , monologue you threw at me when I agreed to be your roommate?"

"Yes, do you recall it?"

Watson cleared his throat, changed his pose, and mimicked Sherlock's voice, "This is my side of the room, that's your side. You can have guests, but let me know first so that I can remove valuable things from the room. You can talk to me if you must, just don't expect the same from me in return. I don't care about your past, you don't want to hear mine I assure you, so don't ask. Got it? Good."

When he was done, Watson went back to his normal stance and looked at Sherlock with a smile. Sherlock was very impressed by this, "Well done. You could've been an actor instead of a doctor."

"I thought about it actually, did a lot of plays when I was younger."

"Why not do it?"

"I wanted to help people in ways that went beyond making them smile or moving them to tears."

"Besides, you do that with your girlfriends for free."

"True enough."

They shared a laugh, then Sherlock went back to his snack, and Watson made to leave, but he stopped himself before he made it to the hallway, "Oh my gosh!"

"What? What's wrong?" asked Sherlock concerned about what may have happened.

"I just realized, I get why you hate Mycroft so much."

This time it was Sherlock who went into a laughing fit, but just as quickly he sobered up and looked at Watson, "Yes, now you know."

"I can't imagine the horrors the two of you inflicted on each other through the years at your house."

"It was...a lot."

"So for the record...you would've let Lucas kill him?"

"I...would've seriously considered it. Let's leave it at that."

With a nod of acknowledgment Watson left, Sherlock finished making the snack he started and bit into it. He relished the taste, "Peanut butter and jelly, glorious."

He picked up his plate and joined Watson in the living room. Watson turned on the TV, while Sherlock finished his sandwich and then went back to reading the paper. All was peaceful, then a knock came at the door.

"Expecting someone? Mary perhaps?" asked Sherlock.

"She's out of town for her job. Might be a client though," thought Watson.

"Oh! ...why didn't I think of that?"

"PB&J melts your brain process."

"We all have our vices Watson, now come on!"

They went to the door, and straightened themselves up before opening it. In their doorway was a woman, looking very desperate in her expression.

"Excuse me, are you Sherlock Holmes? I need your help."

Sherlock quickly examined the woman, she was surprisingly tall, nearly as tall as him. Her outfit was casual, a simple shirt and skirt combination, but she had a light jacket as well. Her hair was long and blonde, well beyond her shoulders, and her eye color were purest blue. However, the area around her eyes were beat red, signaling to Sherlock that she had been crying a lot. The other thing that caught his eye was that her right hand had a vice grip around the purse she was carrying.

He shook off the investigation and motioned for her to enter, "Yes, I am he, please come in."

As she entered, Sherlock shared a look with Watson to signify that this was a serious matter, Watson nodded in acknowledgement. They guided her to the living room, and had her sit in the chair opposite their own.

When she got comfortable Sherlock leaned in, "Please, tell us everything. Starting with your name."

"My name is Dee, and I need your help," she replied.

"With what?" asked Watson, also leaning in.

"It's my brother, he's missing."

The simplicity of this took Sherlock and Watson aback, and they shared an uncertain look, but Sherlock recovered quickly, "That's usually a matter for the police. How long has he been gone?"

"Two days since I last saw him, and I did tell the police. They haven't found a trace of him."

"You're not telling us something, Dee. What are you hiding?"

She grew very uncomfortable at this, and clenched her purse much harder, which got the attention of Sherlock, but he didn't push it. Instead, he let her work out her feelings, and soon she addressed them, "My brother, Kenny, and I were on vacation. We live here in London, but we travel to a different city every year, it's our way of getting out of our routines and having fun together like we did when we were kids."

"That sounds like a wonderful tradition," said Watson with a kind smile.

"It is!" Dee exclaimed with her own smile, "We've been all over Europe together. Big cities, small towns, landmarks, it's wonderful... wonderful..."

She started to tear up, Watson reacted quickly and handed her some nearby tissues, "Here."

"Thank you. Anyway, we were on vacation in this small town a few hours from London. It has a funny history, Kenny always liked those places. We were there for five days without incident. But then, the next day, Kenny went out to go find something...and he never came back."

"What was he looking for?" asked Sherlock curious.

"This landmark, it was tied to the history of the town, he almost forgot about it, and he wanted to see it. I wanted to start packing our things so I told him to go ahead without me..."

Dee cried, and the two let her. Sherlock took the chance to eye the purse, as it had not left her grip.

"I'm sorry, I'm sorry. Um, I waited, and I called him, and I searched for him, and I couldn't find him. I told the police, I even stayed an extra day there, I couldn't find a trace of him. And then..."

She seemed to choke on the words, and her eyes went to her purse, Sherlock knew what to do, "And then...? What did you see?"

"A dog."

Watson got surprised at the statement, "A dog? I don't understand."

"I was searching for Kenny, and I looked across the street, and there was a dog, just walking along the sidewalk. And in his mouth...was this..."

She reached inside her purse, and pulled out a red scarf, it had some scruffs and bite marks on it, but it was mostly intact. Dee seemed almost frightened to hold it in her hands.

Sherlock pieced together the truth, "This is your brothers scarf, isn't it?"

"Yes, but that's not all..."

"What is?" asked Watson, slightly dreading the answer.

"I've never seen that dog before, ever! But I recognized Kenny's scarf, so I shouted at the dog, "Where do you get that scarf?" And...and..."

"And?" urged Sherlock.

"The dog stopped, and looked at me, and then slowly came across the street, and dropped the scarf at my feet. Its expression when it looked back at me. It was...sad...like it knew what happened to Kenny. Then it left. Just like that."

Sherlock and Watson looked at each other flabbergasted, neither not knowing what to make of this news.

Dee became exasperated at their silence, "I'm telling the truth!"

Sherlock held up a hand, "I know, I can tell. That's why you came to us, isn't it? You knew we would believe you?"

She laughed a little, "I'm...a reader of your stories Dr. Watson. You two have been through a lot, the police...they won't go the extra mile to find Kenny, but I know you will. Please help me. Please help me find my brother."

"We will," assured Watson, "right Sherlock?"

"Of course," acknowledged Sherlock with a nod.

Dee smiled, "Thank you. I know to fear the worst because of how long it's been since Kenny's disappearance, but I need to know what happened, either way."

"It's only fair."

"Right, the not knowing is the worst part. But we're going to need your help Dee. Where do you go on vacation with your brother?" asked Watson

Her eyes glazed over as she recalled it, "We went to Baskerville."

At the mention of the name, Watson literally jumped out of his chair in horror. Both Dee and Sherlock were surprised by his reaction, Sherlock most of all, "Watson? What's wrong?"

Watson didn't seem to hear him, he just muttered to himself, "Basker...Baskerville..."

"Watson!"

The shout snapped him back to, "What? What?"

Sherlock rose and went over to him and grabbed his arm, then turned to Dee, "Give us a moment, please."

"Of course," said Dee, not sure of what was going on.

With some force, Sherlock pulled Watson into the chemistry room. He made sure Dee didn't follow them before confronting Watson, "What was that about? I've never seen you react that way."

"It's...complicated," said Watson hesitantly.

"Oh please, what happened to you in Baskerville?"

Watson went wide-eyed, to which Sherlock laughed, "Come on! She said the name and you almost leapt through the ceiling! You've been there before, what happened?"

He got uncomfortable at the question, but straightened himself up quickly and regained his composure, "I'll tell you later."

"Watson..."

"I promise I will tell you, but it's a long story, and we have our client who deserves our attention. Let's tell her we're taking the case and get ready to go. It's a long train ride to Baskerville, I'll tell you then."

"If you don't, I will pester you endlessly until you crack."

Watson chuckled, "Of that I have no doubt."

With a nod to the other, the two left the room and re-entered the living room, Dee was still there, but was rather nervous looking when they came back, "Is...everything alright?"

"Yes," stated Watson blankly, "I have had some dealings in Baskerville myself."

"So you know then?"

"How weird it is? Yeah, I do."

"Will you...are you still going to help me?"

Sherlock looked to Watson, who gave him a nod, to which he smiled then returned his gaze to Dee, "Of course, your brother needs to be found, and we will do everything in our power to find him. And should the worse have happened, find those responsible."

Dee couldn't get the words out, but she nodded in acknowledgement. She gave Sherlock and Watson her contact information, then was guided out by Sherlock.

With haste, they made their preparations to leave. Sherlock focused on the items he might need to find Kenny, as well as any scientific gear he might require to solve any unforeseen obstacles. Watson meanwhile booked their hotel and train tickets, as well as started to pack their clothes.

In an hour they were all ready, and bade Mrs. Hudson goodbye before making their way to the station. They made it just in the nick of time, and boarded the train minutes before it departed. Once on board, they made their way to some empty seats, and watched as the city slowly turned into the countryside. Both Sherlock and Watson were deep in thought, but thinking about entirely different things.

Watson was the first to break from his thoughts, and when he saw Sherlock still pondering he smiled, "What part of the case has you so intrigued?"

"The dog," Sherlock answered bluntly

A shiver flew up Watson's spine, "I should've known you'd say that."

Sherlock noticed how Watson got as uncomfortable as he was in the apartment when Baskerville was brought up, so he leaned in to get his attention, "Alright, we're on the train, and we have a long trip, what happened to you in Baskerville?"

"Ok, ok...I went there on a school trip once..."

"That didn't happen at college."

"Not college, school, like grade school."

"What school takes young children so far away from home?" asked Sherlock perplexed.

Watson laughed ironically, "One that appreciates history. Don't you remember when and how Baskerville was founded?

"Oh, right. It was founded after the war."

"THE war, World War I. The original Baskervilles lost their village in one of the major battles. So, they decided to rebuild, and they did it on the site of another battle, a smaller one mind you. They spent a year cleaning it up, making it livable. But they did it."

"People flocked to this peaceful little village if I recall correctly."

With a nod, Watson turned his attention away from Sherlock and looked out the window, where rolling hills were now in view, "The people who came named the village after them, thus Baskerville was born. Then World War II happened."

Sherlock leaned in more, now very intrigued, "I'll admit, I'm a little rusty on the history of the village. What happened?"

"Nearly the whole family got wiped out in the war. The village was untouched, no one knows how the Germans' missed it, but they did. However, nearly the whole line of Baskervilles was wiped out, save for the youngest son. He came back home, and that's when things started...happening."

"Happening?"

"I don't know myself. But reports say that things in the village became...unnatural. Disappearances, odd deaths, things that didn't add up to the police. Then, in the early 80's the military was given permission to set up a science lab there. It burned down one day. No one knows why. Ever since, the village has been given the titles of "weird" and "mysterious", yet no one denied the history that it had carved for itself. So...schools go there often."

"So what happened on yours?"

Watson turned to Sherlock, but then looked back outside, on the hills he stared at, a young boy faded in from his mind, it was him from so long ago. He watched as the young version of himself ran on the hills.

"I was ten when we did the trip. Long after the military facility fire mind you. Things had apparently quieted down in the town, so the school thought it would be a nice trip to take us on. It was a lovely day, the forest was glistening, the animals were all amazing to look at. And...I saw a cat."

"A cat?" asked Sherlock, not sure of the significance.

"I liked animals a lot when I was a kid. This cat was a type I had never seen before, so...I chased after it."

"I'm sure Mary would think that was adorable."

"Shut up, Sherlock."

He focused back on the vision of his younger self, this time though he was chasing a orange tabby cat. Watson shook his head at the younger version of himself, knowing what was to come.

"I still remember my teachers yelling at me to get back in the group, but I wanted that cat, so I kept going after it. The cat went through a log, and I went in after it. Almost got stuck, by the time I wiggled my way out...it was gone, and I found myself very lost."

Sherlock was surprised by the turn of events, "That must have been terrifying."

"For a ten year old? You bet, especially when you have a wide view of the area, and you can't see the people you came with."

"So what did you do?"

"I didn't panic if that's the answer you're looking for. ...that was the answer you were looking for, wasn't it?"

"Maybe."

"I hate you."

"I know, but please continue."

Watson rolled his eyes, "Thankfully, I kept my cool, and I sat on the log I crawled out of and waited for someone to appear. A few minutes passed and I saw something...but it wasn't what I was expecting."

Again, he turned to the window, and he saw his younger self sitting on a log, afraid, but keeping somewhat calm. Soon, a shadow appeared on the ground, engulfing the young Watson's shadow, and making him turn around in rejoice. But his expression soon turned to fear.

"What did you see?" asked Sherlock.

"A hound."

"What?"

"A bloodhound, Sherlock."

The young Watson was now starring at a bloodhound. One of impressive size, whose eyes were level with Watsons. The dog looked at Watson, who looked right back at the dog.

"What did you do?"

"At first? Nothing. I wasn't sure what to do, the dog had no tags, meant it was wild, so I froze."

"I'm sensing a twist."

"Yes, there is a twist."

The young Watson kept frozen in posture and expression, but soon, he relaxed as the dog made no menacing motions to him. Watson then smiled at the dog. To which, the dog smiled back in a very unnatural way.

"It smiled?" blurted out Sherlock in disbelief.

"It smiled. In a very, very, human way." said Watson with a touch of fear, "So naturally, I ran as fast as I could. I thought for sure it would chase me, but it didn't, didn't even howl or bark. I eventually caught up to my class. Told them about the dog. No one believed me obviously."

"A dog smiling like a human? Hard to believe. For most anyway."

Watson turned to Sherlock, expression curious, "So you believe me?"

Sherlock nodded with confidence and sincerity, "Of course, what possible reason do you have to lie? Plus, this is now the second dog from the area of Baskerville that has exhibited human like behavior."

"The dog with the scarf! What didn't I connect that?"

"Because you heard about Baskerville after the news about the dog, your mind was elsewhere."

"Fair enough. What does this all mean Sherlock?"

Sherlock sighed heavily, then looked out the window himself, "It means there's a lot going on in the village known as Baskerville, and we had better be careful in it."

Chapter Two: An Odd Welcome

Sometime later, the train pulled into a station. Sherlock and Watson disembarked once it came to a stop.. After securing their bags they quickly made for the entrance of the station so that they could see the village itself. Almost immediately, Sherlock began observing everyone and everything that was around him. Looking for any information and clues that could be of value.

They soon made it to the entrance of the station, and once they were outside, they took notice of the village of Baskerville.

Despite the modern time they were in, the village looked very much like an older version of the world. There were modern amenities to be sure. Cars, people on cell phones and tablets, etc., but the architecture was more old-fashioned. Even the buildings that were clearly constructed recently had an older look to them due to what they were made out of.

Watson was on edge as he looked around, but couldn't help but laugh at the irony, "Amazing, it's barely changed in 20 years."

Sherlock turned, "What has changed?"

"Size. I could tell coming in that the village is bigger than before. Maybe double? Still though, not that big in comparison to London."

"Heh, few things are."

"True. So, shall we head to the hotel?"

"Yes, let's settle before we explore," Sherlock said after a moments' pause.

"I'll lead the way, I have the map to it on my phone."

He pulled out his phone and typed on it a few times. Once he had it, he motioned for Sherlock to follow. They passed down several streets as they made their way deeper into the village. While Watson focused on the streets they were turning on, and the instructions on his phone,

Sherlock was again glancing at all the people that they passed by. An uncertain expression grew on Sherlock's face with each person that they passed.

A few minutes later they reached a small inn. A sign hung from a pole mounted in the wall, it read, "The Doghouse."

Sherlock couldn't help but laugh at that, "Seriously? After that story you told me, you booked us here?"

Watson groaned, "It's the only inn here Sherlock, and we got lucky, there was only one room available. How much do you want to bet it was Dee and Kenny's?"

"Hmm...let's hope it is. It might have some clues as to his disappearance. Potentially of course, it's no doubt been cleaned. Regardless, let's go in."

He marched into the doorway, Watson followed. Once inside, the two looked around at the inside of the inn. It was very proper, and had a stylish wood feel to everything that wasn't stone and brick. There were wood counters, floors, and of course, tables and chairs. The two were both impressed by the charm of the room.

As Watson admired it, he soon eyed the service desk, and nudged Sherlock to follow him to it. As they approached, a young red-headed girl appeared from behind a door.

"Hello!" she said happily and with a kind smile, "Welcome to the Doghouse! How may I help you?"

Watson got her attention with a wave of the hand, "Hello. My name is John Watson, we have a reservation."

"Ok!"

The girl quickly typed on the computer, her head bobbed as she did. She beamed when she was done, "Found it! We're still cleaning it up from the last user. Would you mind waiting a little while?"

"How long do you think?"

"Hour, maybe two. We can hold your bags here and put them in your rooms when it's ready. I'll even give you the key cards now if you want!"

Sherlock fought to hold back a laugh at the energy the girl had, a glare from Watson settled him down though, "That would be lovely. We only have the two bags here."

"Ok!" exclaimed the girl, who basically skipped around the counter towards them and tagged their luggage. She then went back to her computer and typed quickly on it, then two put two key cards on the counter, "These are for you! Your room number is 11, and is down that hall. Enjoy your stay in Baskerville!"

"We will do our best. Thank you."

"Bye-bye!"

She waved and smiled at them as they left. Watson made sure Sherlock got out the door first, then promptly closed the door, "Alright, get it out of your system."

Sherlock immediately burst out laughing, and mocked the girl behind the desk by mimicking her gestures and expressions. Some passerby's saw this and were confused. Watson apologized to them for Sherlock's behavior. Soon though, Sherlock calmed down.

Watson though was not amused, "Are you done?"

"Yes," replied Sherlock after a few more laughs and snorts.

"I know you love judging people for their personalities, but what was wrong with that girl? She was trying to be kind and courteous."

"She was trying to be a cartoon character. The skipping, the loud voice, dear gosh I fear for the next generation. Absorbed in their technology, not learning real life lessons."

"That girl is no older than 16 and already has a job. How's that not a good life lesson?"

With a raise of the hand, Sherlock made to retort, but he thought about what Watson said and went into a more thoughtful pose, "Hmm, good point. Her personality was odd though."

"Don't we all have odd personalities?"

"Touché, Watson. Now that that's done, shall we focus on the case?"

Watson nodded, "Yes, did you see anything interesting while we walked here."

Sherlock's expression grew grim, "Yes, and you're not going to like it."

"What?"

"The people here, they looked at us when we walked by."

"So? It's clear we're tourists...well, kind of tourists. Why should that matter?"

He stepped closer to Watson to ensure that no one else heard him, "They looked at us like we were dead men walking."

Watson's eyes went wide at this, and he fought the urge to look around, "Ok, so we're either in danger, or they know what's going on. Or both. What should we do first? Look for Kenny? Maybe look for that dog that Dee saw?"

This caused Sherlock to chuckle, "That's going to be difficult Watson. Look around, slowly."

Heeding his advice, Watson carefully gazed around the area, to his amazement, there were loads of dogs roaming around the town. Some were with people, others were just walking of their own free will. The sheer volume of them made his jaw drop a little, "My word."

"Indeed. The people of Baskerville seem to really like their dogs. Our work just got a lot more difficult on one end. However, we do need to go look for Kenny, as that's our primary goal. I suggest we go to the local police and see if they have any files on these disappearance. Any information is useful information."

"Sounds like a plan. I think we passed their station on the way over. Let's go."

With haste, they made their way down the street, being careful of course to not draw too much attention to themselves. Unbeknownst to them, in a nearby alley, the dog that gave Dee the scarf was watching them intently.

Within a few minutes they made it to the station. It was very simple, much like all the other buildings in the town. It too had a sign showing what it was, making Sherlock look at it in scrutiny when it caught his eye. His glare intensified with each second he stared at it.

Watson saw this and tapped him on the shoulder, "Sherlock?"

He quickly snapped out of it, "Hmm? Oh, sorry, a realization just hit me. We're going to have to take a different approach here. Follow my lead?"

"Are you asking me that because you're about to insult a lot of people?"

"Actually, no, I can honestly say that won't help here."

Sherlock smiled to show he meant it, but Watson was unconvinced, he shook his head and sighed though, "Ok, I'll follow your lead. Don't blow this Sherlock, you know why we're here."

"I'd be a fool to forget."

He motioned for Watson to actually go in ahead of him, to which Watson did, but the moment the door was fully opened a bark made him jump backwards. Hitting Sherlock and almost knocking them both down in the process.

As they kept their positions they both looked upon a massive Rottweiler, it was attached to a desk via a chain, but was desperately trying to reach them.

"Rex! You darn dog, stop scaring the people!" came a voice.

The two turned to see a slightly heavyset police officer coming over to the dog and quickly calming him down. Though the dog went quiet, its eyes were still glued on Sherlock and Watson.

Job done, the man then approached Sherlock and Watson, and extended a hand to them, and they both shook it after righting themselves, "Sergeant Myers, Baskerville PD...heh...if you call it that."

"We few, we proud few..." called out another voice, and they saw another officer sitting behind a nearby desk, he raised a coffee mug to them as they looked to him.

"Right you are Jay. Anyway, sorry about Rex, he's very peculiar, he can somehow tell who isn't from here and barks at them like they're the enemy."

"Yes...quite...peculiar..." said Watson, eyes going back to the dog.

"Don't worry, he hasn't broken that chain since I got it two years ago. You'll be fine. So, you're clearly new, how I may help you?"

Sherlock got in front of Watson and put on a happy-go-lucky expression, even lightened his voice a bit to sell the impression he wanted to give them, "Yes, hello, I'm Sherlock, this is my friend John Watson. We're tourists from London, and we could use some advice, dear officer."

He smiled kindly at Myers, which took Watson aback for a bit but he recovered and added his own smile to the mix. Myers seemed happy to be needed, "Well, of course! Our history may be "odd" but that doesn't mean we can't be helpful! Right Jay?"

"Yep." Jay replied, again raising his glass.

"Exactly, so what advice you need?"

"Well, a friend of ours was here recently and recommended some wonderful spots to visit, but they failed to mention the grandness and scope that this supposedly small village has! We don't want to step on anyone's toes or anything, so we were wondering, is there places we should avoid? Dangerous spots that we can get hurt in? I don't want to lead my dear friend astray on what's supposed to be an adventure of sorts."

This sobered up Myers, and it seemed like he was fighting back tears, "Such compassion, such caring. You are a good man, and you are lucky to have him as your friend."

"I can't tell you ways I'm lucky in regards to Sherlock," said Watson, struggling to not sound sarcastic.

"If more people were like him, we wouldn't have our "dark" history!" noted Jay with a chuckle.

Myers scoffed at that, "That's a joke! Baskerville is always going to be this way. Now, as for your question, follow me."

He guided them over to his desk. Sherlock's eyes immediately scanned as many papers that were on it as he could, trying to get any information from them. Soon, they were all covered by a map, and Sherlock returned to his kind expression and demeanor to not draw attention to himself.

"So, here's the town, here's where you are now. I recommend going to the hills, the statue lane, all hand-crafted, very artsy."

"You'd like that Watson," nudged Sherlock.

"I do appreciate art made by hands, I am a doctor after all." he stated with a smirk.

"Oh, it's very popular," noted Myers, "lots of tourists go there. Now, as where not to go. This area is a little shady. Every town has criminals, even Baskerville. Speaking of which, the mansion here? Don't go there. That's the Baskerville residence."

"Why can't we go there? Is it haunted?" asked Sherlock in a dramatic voice

"No, but Sir Baskerville doesn't like to be disturbed."

Watson chuckled, "Oh I can understand...wait, a Baskerville is still alive?"

"Watson," said Sherlock feigning disappointment, "of course the Baskervilles still live! The family didn't die out! I believe it is Sir Rudolph Baskerville who resides there, is that correct Sergeant?"

Myers gave a thumbs up to show he was indeed correct, "Very nice, and don't worry sonny, Sir Baskerville doesn't advertise his existence, or that he lives in the family mansion, he prefers it that way."

"Noted." acknowledged Watson

"Ok, where else not to go..."

Sherlock leaned in towards the map, "What about the forest?"

"Oh no, don't get there. That's really dangerous."

"Why?"

"Look at the map, the forest is huge. Easy to get lost if you're not skilled in keeping track of where you're going. Plus, there's wild things there."

"Wild things?"

He pointed to Rex, who was eyeing them still, "All the dogs in town? They're tamed. But there are wild ones in the forest. No one knows where they came from, but they're there, and they will attack. Being frank with you, if you got lost in there, you're on your own. We're not equipped to deal with what goes on in there."

Jay chuckled, "Frank? I thought your name was Ray!"

He laughed even harder after the joke was made, making Myers roll his eyes, "Oh yeah, haven't heard that one before...oh wait, I have! Every time I use that expression!"

The two got into a minor spat, Sherlock used the opportunity to memorize the map and all its landmarks, including the outlying areas that he felt he should know. Watson kept eyes on the officers, nudging Sherlock when Myers returned his attention to them.

"Sorry about that, any other questions?"

Sherlock smiled and shook his head, "Nope, you've given me all the answers we need. If we have any more questions, we'll be sure to ask. Good day to you."

With a small bow, he turned and left, Watson was surprised by this, but followed suit. They soon went out the door, but Sherlock didn't stop walking until they were in a nearby alley.

Once clear of listeners, Watson looked at Sherlock with clear confusion, "What was that about? You didn't ask about Kenny or any of the other incidents that happened here!"

Sherlock's more focused expression returned to his face, "I know, a thought came to mind when I saw the sign. How is it the police have no clue as to what's going on here? Disappearances, weird accidents, potentially dead people, how could that happen? Are they inept? Paid off? What?"

"Your conclusion based on what we saw?"

"They could be both, it's hard to say. But I realize now based on how obvious it is that we are strangers here, if we start asking the wrong questions, we're never going to get any answers at all."

"That's feels right, small town mentality. Haven't had to deal with that before. Not unless you count that dorm mentality we had to fight once."

This made Sherlock recall a case, "Hmm, good parallel Watson, those fraternity brothers did have a tight code. This town might have that too. We'll need to be careful."

"Indeed, but Sherlock, we need that information. We can't just do this blind, we wouldn't know where to start!"

"Right you are, which is why when night falls, we're going to break into the police building and scan the files ourselves."

Sherlock seemed proud of his answer, yet Watson was unmoved, in fact, he couldn't believe Sherlock said that, "You just said that the best plan was to not ask the wrong questions, and now you want to break into a building?"

"Like you said, we need information, and if the town won't give it to us, we'll have to take it. Now can I count on you or not?"

Watson groaned angrily, for numerous reasons, "Yes, I'm with you. But you better hope that the dog isn't in the room when we break in! Cause if it is? I'm out!"

"Noted. Now, let's do what tourists do and roam around. Might draw away some suspicion from us."

"Plus, we might see something that'll help us later."

Sherlock smiled, impressed with the foresight, "Right you are. Ok, let's go."

With that, they made their way back onto the street, and did their best to blend into the town.

Chapter Three: The Things We Find At Night

Night fell a few hours later. Sherlock and Watson remained in their hotel room though. They wanted to be sure that the hour was so late that few would be out at the time. It was around one in the morning when Sherlock nudged a sleeping Watson, "Watson, it's time, get up."

Watson rubbed his eyes and stretched out, "Sorry, sorry, was really tired."

"I know, no worries, I wanted you to sleep at least a little. It's actually been proven that short naps are better than going on no sleep."

"Yeah, read that in school. So, are we going?"

Sherlock nodded, but didn't head for the door. Instead, he grabbed a nearby chair and put it up against the wall so that it sat beneath the hotel window. Watson looked at him in disbelief, "You can't be serious."

"If we go out the front door Watson, there's a good chance we'll be heard. We can't risk that. Just outside the window is a grassy area, so we won't be heard when we plop down, now shut up and come on!"

Sherlock carefully opened the window. It was small, but big enough for him to get through with some effort. Watson watched as he got through it, then groaned and followed suit. Sherlock helped him get out the window and onto the ground with little noise. Now outside, they stood still to ensure that no one heard them. Once they felt they were clear they slowly made their way down the street and towards the police station.

At every street corner they made sure to look out and see if anyone was about. A few times they did see someone, so they remained hidden until they passed by or went into a building.

Step by step, and street by street, they made their way across Baskerville. Until once again they were in front of the Police Station. Both of them looked around to make sure no one was nearby. Then, Sherlock grabbed some tools to pick the door lock. Before he could insert them though, Watson grabbed his arm.

"What?" asked Sherlock confused.

Watson gazed at him in disbelief, but whispered angrily, "The dog!"

"Oh, right, sorry."

Sherlock put the tools on the ground and grabbed something else out of his pocket, and showed it to Watson with a smile.

"Ta-da."

"A whistle, are you insane?"

"Watson, please, it's a dog whistle. Inaudible to all but those who can hear at certain frequencies, like dogs."

He gave a mock clap of appreciation, "Brilliant, but did you forget we're in a town full of dogs? I'm surprised we didn't run into any while we came here!"

This notion put Sherlock into a thoughtful pause, "You're right...where are they? Not all those dogs had human owners, so why aren't they wandering around?"

"Dogs have to sleep too Sherlock."

"True, but something doesn't feel right about that...another matter to figure out. Anyway, this whistle is short range, only about 10 feet in diameter. Which is perfect for where we are right now. If we hear a bark? We know the dog's in there and we'll figure out another plan. Be ready to run just in case, alright?"

"I hate you."

"I know. Here we go."

Sherlock took a breath and blew into the whistle for a good amount of time. To Watson's surprise, no barking came forth, the night remained quiet. Sherlock stopped and smiled, "Wonderful, one of the officers must have taken the dog home. Let's get in, quickly."

He grabbed his lockpicking tools and quickly opened the door, smirking as he did so, "Take that, Lucas."

"You know he can't hear you, right?"

"You never know, his hearing is clearly above average. Now come on."

Carefully, they entered the room. Both Sherlock and Watson looked for any sign of a security system, but to their relief, they found none. They did their best to not make a sound as they walked through the room and towards the filing cabinets.

Once they reached them, Sherlock pointed out that they were locked. This didn't seem to faze Watson, "Why wouldn't they be locked? We're in a police station!"

"Yes, but one that already has a locked door? And one where everyone knows everyone?"

"Maybe, but remember, Myers said there was a criminal element here."

"True, still, feels weird."

"Just open it, will you?"

With haste, Sherlock again picked the lock, and carefully opened the top drawer of the cabinet. He quickly thumbed through the files, but the more he did, the more confused his look got.

Watson noted this and got confused himself, "What?"

"No criminal reports in this one. It's profiles of the people here."

"What?"

"I don't know...something is very wrong."

He moved to the next drawer, and sighed with relief at what he saw, "Finally, criminal reports. Here is Kenny's!"

With a rush, Sherlock pulled it out and looked over it. Watson waited patiently for his analysis, but noticed Sherlock's expression go from excited to find it, to confusion, to downright stupor, to the point where his jaw dropped.

"What's wrong?" asked Watson confused.

"There's barely anything here!" Sherlock exclaimed, "Look!"

He gave the file to Watson, who then looked it over himself. The file did have heft to it, however, as he flipped through the pages, the next page had less on it than the last, until he was literally flipping through blank pages, "What in the world?"

"Exactly. The first few pages are an actual report, but everything else after that is scribbles and dribble. That file was made to make people think they were investigating."

"Why wouldn't the police want to investigate the disappearance? Aren't they afraid of the attention?"

Sherlock thought about it, then chuckled, "Maybe that's why they don't."

Watson shook his head in confusion, "I'm sorry?"

"You said it yourself, Watson. Baskerville has a reputation, weird things happen here. So maybe...they feel they don't need to investigate. For a death or disappearance would be chalked up to the towns "history"."

"We've seen stranger, however, we can't deny your other notion, that the police are involved in whatever's happening."

"Very true. Let me see the file again."

Watson gave it to Sherlock, who went over the first few pages again. Like last time though, a confused look came on his face, but this one was more inquisitive. He held the file out for Watson to see, "What do you make of these acronyms?"

"Let's see...D.N.S., and P.F.H., they don't ring a bell. Certainly not a medical term. What do you think?

Sherlock closed his eyes and took a deep breath, then slowly went over every possible combination of word that the acronyms could mean. Words flew in and out of his mind, and he mouthed every sequence that came through it. Watson watched with a smile as he did this.

Eventually, Sherlock stopped, and sighed, "Blast."

"Nothing?" wondered Watson.

"Worse, everything. There are plenty of possible combinations that the acronyms could be, each of which could mean one thing or another that's happening in this town."

"Do you have any that stick out to you?"

"Maybe. Notice that D.N.S. is next to the 'Status' column of the police report. Which is labeled, 'Missing', in Kenny's case. It could mean 'Do Not Search'. But I'm not sure."

"'Do Not Search'? Like, don't search him if found?"

"More like, don't search for him, at all."

"So the police are in on it?"

Sherlock sighed angrily and threw the file on the nearest desk, "I don't know! Like I said, this was just one possibility for what it meant. It's strong in likelihood, but that's all it is. We don't have enough to prove anything yet."

Watson watched Sherlock for a bit, then went to the drawer with the criminal reports and began to strum through them. Sherlock heard this and turned to him.

"What are you doing?"

"Well, just because we can't prove anything for Kenny doesn't mean we can't prove anything. If there is something going on here, how much do you want to bet that it involves more people?"

The wheels began to turn in Sherlock's head, "A serial killing, on an impressive scale."

"Something like that. It has to be. So, let's see how many other 'missing' or 'accidental death' cases there are, and we'll go from there," purposed Watson.

"Great idea, Watson. Get out your phone, we'll take pictures of the front pages and look over them in the hotel room. We shouldn't dawdle here any longer than we have to."

"Agreed, let's go."

With haste, they raced through the rest of the files, pulling out ones that were of interest to them. Once separated, both Sherlock and Watson took photos of the pages of interest, making sure they were in good quality so that they could be read later.

Once done, Sherlock used his memory to put everything back in its proper order. They quickly looked at the room to ensure that nothing was out of place. Assured they were in the clear, they slowly opened the door and peeked out into the street to see if anyone was out there. No one entered their view, so they exited, making sure they locked the door as they left.

Now out onto the street, they carefully made their way to the nearest alley, and then made for the hotel. As they did though, the dog from before peaked out from the shadows of another alley, eyes fixed on them as they made their getaway.

Back at the hotel, Sherlock and Watson transferred the pictures they took on their phones to a laptop. Once there, Sherlock separated them by date and case type. Sherlock's eyes darted from side to side as he clicked on picture after picture trying to decide what was important and what wasn't. Watson waited patiently as he did so.

Soon, Sherlock closed his eyes and sighed, Watson knew he was done and asked, "Well?"

"Something is going on, but I don't know what," he replied grimly.

"Best guess?"

"Either there's a serial killer, or this town is well and truly cursed to those who come to visit it."

"That's not funny."

"I'm serious. Look."

He brought up a few of the pictures and spun the laptop around so Watson could see, to which he quickly scrolled through them "What am I looking at?"

"These reports were some of the oldest we found, that drawer only kept files going back a few years. An oddity in and of itself. Notice that some of these ones happened within months of each other, while others have a larger gap. There's no pattern to the disappearances or potential killings."

Watson shivered, "That's disheartening."

"Exactly, and if this was a simple case of wild dogs, the town would warn against going into the woods, like what Myers did with us. Not everyone is a troublemaker, and there's been no sign of foul play with the dogs within the town. So..."

"How did they get to where the dogs are in the woods? And if the dogs aren't the cause, what is?"

Sherlock gave a knowing point to indicate he was on the right track. Watson sighed and went towards the window, the faint outline of the forest could be seen through it.

"I hate this place."

"How grim, Watson," teased Sherlock.

"I'm serious. My personal experience aside, something just feels off about this place. You said yourself that the people were eyeing us the moment we got here, and I can't... I can't shake the feeling that we're being watched."

"You felt it too? Interesting. Well, whoever is watching us will regret it when we find them. But for now, we need to plan our next move."

"Which is?" Watson asked as he moved back towards Sherlock.

Sherlock leaned back in his chair a bit and looked at the ceiling. His thoughts swirling as he gazed at the somewhat intricate design of the ceilings material.

Soon enough he returned to flat footing and stood to face Watson, "Well, if we can't trust the common folk, and we can't trust the police, then there's only one group we can trust."

"Out-of-towners?"

"Good guess, but not correct under these circumstances. I'm talking about the underworld of Baskerville."

Watson scoffed, "You want us to talk to the criminals here?"

"Why not? If this town is in on the secret, that means they trust one another, but who would trust a criminal with keeping such a grand secret? No one. So, we ask them."

"This won't end well."

"Perhaps, but right now? We have no other options. We need more information, and your misgivings aside, they might know something."

Watson sighed angrily, his foot tapped the floor anxiously. After a few moments of thought though he calmed himself and nodded, "You're right. But we're going in daylight!"

Sherlock smiled, "Of course, even criminals need to sleep, and so do we. Let's rest up, tomorrow we need to do our best to find out what's going on, one way or another."

Chapter Four: Town Secrets

Morning came, Sherlock and Watson awoke from their sleep rested, but nervous. They both knew that today was very important for their investigation, and that if things didn't start to fall in line, it might all fall apart.

To ensure that suspicion didn't fall onto them too quickly, they ate breakfast at the inn, then spent the early hours of the morning roaming around town to see some of the sights like tourists would do. Sherlock noticed people still eyeing them, but not as many as before, which led him to believe that their ruse was working.

As the sun rose into the middle of the sky, Sherlock pulled Watson into a side alley.

"I think that's enough diversion," noted Sherlock with a casual glance back towards the main street to see if anyone had followed them or were watching them. "I think it's time we met the criminal element. Are you ready?"

"Quite," said Watson firmly.

"Are you alright?"

"I'm fine, but I'm also ready in case they try something."

This caused Sherlock to pause, the intent of Watson's words made him uneasy, but it wasn't enough to give meaning as to what he meant. Watson's body language and expression didn't give him any clues either, so he was forced to nod hesitantly, then head down the alleyway.

With Sherlock in the lead they made their way through the town's back alleys. As they did, Watson noticed how the quality of the town slowly deteriorated the farther they went down this path. As they made their way onto less kept roads, shadowy figures began to appear around them. Both Sherlock and Watson tensed up, but kept going down their path.

Eventually, they made their way to an alley, one that was a dead end. When they turned around to leave though, they found the pathway blocked by a group of men.

Each of them were looking at the two with evil smiles and hungry eyes.

From the middle of this pack a man stepped forward, he held a knife in one hand, and an apple in the other. As he made his way towards Sherlock and Watson he began to skin the apple, "You blokes are in the wrong part of town."

"Are we?" said Sherlock feigning ignorance.

"Yes, you are. This part of Baskerville belongs to us, which means you have to pay the toll to get by. We'll start with whatever is in your wallets."

"I don't think so," said Watson defiantly, fire in his eyes.

The man laughed, which caused the others to join in, "Ah, this one has guts. Good, that makes it more fun."

"You take one more step towards me and you'll regret it."

One of the men in the back whistled, which started another wave of laughs. The man with the knife took a bite out of the apple and eyed Watson for a bit, then took a step forward, "Now you listen--"

Quick as a flash, Watson kicked the man's knee, forcing him to spin around, before the others could react, Watson put the man in a headlock, then with his other hand pulled out a gun and put it to his head.

"Back off!" said Watson to the other men as they made to free their leader, "Not one more step!"

The men looked at him unnerved, but they weren't the only ones. Sherlock was looking at Watson in shock, not expecting him to do anything like that.

Watson meanwhile focused back on the man in his grasp, "Now you listen to me, we know there's something going on in this town, and we're here to find out what, and stop it. You have two options. Help us, or get out of our way. Honest tip though? I suggest you help."

He cocked the gun quickly and put it back on the man's head to show he meant business. Uneasy, but knowing he didn't have a choice, the man motioned his crew to take it easy. They reluctantly did so.

"Ok, I'll tell you what I know," he said, "just let me go."

"You try anything? Well, use your imagination."

With precision, Watson released the man and pushed him away so that he couldn't try a fast one and strike back at him. He kept the gun trained on him though, to show he meant business. Sherlock's eyes were still glued to Watson, but he shook himself back into focus after the man was freed.

"We weren't expecting such a quick arrival from you," admitted Sherlock, "but now that we're here, let's talk business. Mainly, the business of death. What's going on in this town?"

The man chuckled, "The town's got a history, everyone knows that."

"True, but not to this extent. Wild dogs potentially killing people. Decades worth of "accidents" and missing tourists? That's more than just history, that's a pattern."

"We didn't do it, if that's what you're asking."

"It's not. But we have a feeling you know something. So, please, tell us."

The man looked at his crew, then eyed Watson, who hadn't lowered his stance with his gun. The leader rubbed his neck a bit before pacing in front of his men.

"No one knows when it started," he said grimly

"When what started?" asked Watson intensely.

"The disappearances. Big cities, small towns, people disappear, that's the rule. It happens. Soon, people started noticing that it was happening more and more frequently. Some within a few months, some within weeks, it just depended."

"On what?"

"Don't know."

"Then tell us something you do!"

"Baskerville."

Sherlock looked at the man curiously, "The town?"

"The person," he corrected, "there's one rule in this town that's supposed to be absolute. No one goes to Baskerville Manor. Yet, me and my boys have seen many groups over the years go to the Manor in the dead of night. A few days later? Someone disappears."

"Are you saying they're responsible?"

"No, I'm saying they're someone you should talk to. Be careful when you do though, bring that gun, you might need it."

Watson tightened his grip on the gun, but Sherlock put his hand on it and pushed it down. Reluctantly, Watson dropped his stance.

"What about the dogs?" asked Sherlock.

The man smiled, "What about them?"

"They're connected, I can tell, how?"

"I don't know. The dogs are a part of the town, have been since after World War II. They live in the forest, live in the town, here one minute, gone the next. Where do they come from? Where do they go? In this town, very few know."

This got a laugh out of all of them, save for Sherlock and Watson, who became very uneasy at this.

"Let's go Sherlock," urged Watson.

He nodded, "Right. We do thank you for your help."

The man scoffed, "Please, you won't solve anything. Though when you disappear, I'll be sure to send flowers to your loved ones...eventually."

Watson made a move towards the man, but Sherlock stopped him again, "Enough Watson. We got what we needed, let's go. By your leave of course, good sir."

The man whistled, and the group split in two so that Sherlock and Watson could get by. They slowly did so, making sure that they maintained eye contact with them all to ensure a blindside didn't occur. Once out of range they made for the main roads, keeping an eye out for any tricks.

After a while, they relaxed, and Watson put his gun away, "Well that was a waste of--"

Without warning, Sherlock grabbed Watson by the coat and slammed him against the wall, "What were you thinking pulling that gun?"

Watson was stunned at first, but soon recovered, "I told you that I would be ready if they tried something, and it was a good thing I had it! In case you didn't notice, one had a knife, and who knows what the others had!"

"I was going to handle this with precision, Watson! To barter with them, we're lucky we got anything at all with you threatening them at gunpoint! Where did you even get that gun?"

At the question, Watson became confused, then he laughed, which made Sherlock confused.

"Is something funny, Watson?"

"Yes!" he replied, still laughing, "Are you telling me you didn't know I had that gun?"

"Why would I know you had a gun? Why would I even suspect that?"

"Because it's you! You, who could always tell if I had my wallet on me or not. You, who could tell by my body language whenever I had a breakup. Yet you couldn't tell I had that gun on me?"

Watson laughed even louder at this, but Sherlock was not amused. He released Watson from his grip and looked at him displeased, "I fail to see the humor in me not noticing my friend had gone over the bend."

This sobered Watson up, "I'm not crazy, nor homicidal. But this town? Whatever it is? It's dangerous, more dangerous than any place we've been too before. I felt we needed an extra bit of protection, so I brought it. As for where I got it, it's from that thug that Lucas killed."

"You kept a likely illegal firearm?"

"Yes, but it's not illegal now. After we caught the Wind Fish I had it officially registered. I went through all the proper channels, made sure it wasn't tied to any unsolved cases. Don't forget, I'm a great shot."

"True, but I also know you don't like to show it. Exigent circumstances aside," noted Sherlock with heavy emphasis on the final sentence.

The two stared down the other, both waiting for the other to say something.

Watson was the first to break the silence, but he maintained his intense expression, "If you're looking for an apology, you're not going to get it. Things are changing Sherlock. We're being put into more active cases, dangerous ones. If we're not prepared to defend ourselves for what's coming, we will die. I most definitely don't want to die here, so I brought the gun. Before this is over? I bet it'll save our lives again. Now, are we going to move on? Or shall we continue this row?"

Sherlock continued to glare at Watson, who matched his expression. But, Sherlock soon relented, and nodded in acknowledgement of Watson's statement, "You're right. Things are getting more dangerous, perhaps it is necessary to be more armed. But please Watson, keep your emotions in check when you bring that out. We don't want an accident with it."

This time Watson nodded in acknowledgement of Sherlock's statement, "Of course, I apologize for being a bit rash earlier."

"Bah, they did have it coming."

The two laughed and relaxed in their postures.

"Now Watson, let us go."

"Where?"

"Where else? Baskerville Manor. "

"You believed that bit about groups of people going up to the Manor before a disappearance happened?"

Sherlock shrugged, "I see no reason to doubt them. Why lie about something so specifically? Also, the Manor is close to the forest."

Watson strummed his chin as he processed this, "I guess any lead is a good lead at this point."

"Right you are. Let's go."

After a quick scan of the area around them, the two again made for the main road in town. Yet, once again, as they left, the dog that had been following them appeared again. This time though, it dashed away once they were out of sight.

Quickly, yet carefully, Sherlock and Watson made their way through the town. They tried to act as naturally as they could under the circumstances. The two would start up a random conversation, point at things to make them seem like they were in awe of something , say out loud where they might go next, whatever they felt would draw attention away from them.

As they made their way to the eastern part of town, they noticed a large house beginning to grow in the distance. From the center of town you wouldn't have been able to notice it, but on the outskirts, it was nearly impossible to miss.

The house continued to grow in size as they got closer to it, to the point where both Sherlock and Watson had their jaws drop as the true scope of it came into view.

"Are you kidding me?" asked Watson dumbfounded.

"If only," joked Sherlock.

"How did we not notice this in town?"

"The town has quite a few tall buildings. Plus, there are hills to help block this, and the train we took brought us in the from the west, if we came from the east this would've been in view for some time."

"Fair enough."

With that, they continued their trek to the mansion. A stone path soon appeared at their feet, and they followed it up to the main entranceway. Both Sherlock and Watson stopped to admire the craftsmanship that was put into the Manor. The entranceway itself was very elegant, with carvings of both men and dogs laced into wood and stone. The rest was very much like a mural.

"This must have taken some time to construct," noted Sherlock in admiration of the artwork.

"Agreed, but, given that this family is wealthy, they've could've hired many people to work on it at once."

"Excellent point Watson, I deduce that with a group of fifty artists they could've...could've..."

His gaze wandered from the entranceway towards Watson, and then, to what was behind Watson. On a nearby hill a hundred feet away was a dog. The same dog that had been following them since they arrived in town. Sherlock looked at the dog curiously, and the dog seemed to do the same.

Watson turned to see what Sherlock was looking at, and was taken aback when he saw the dog, "Sherlock, do you think it's one of the wild ones?"

"Hard to say. It's not attacking, it's more like it's...examining us."

"What breed is that? I don't recognize it."

"It's a Belgian Malinois."

"Do I even want to know how you know that?"

"Probably not."

The two continued to stare at the Malinois, and vice versa. After about a minute of staring, the dog turned and walked away.

Sherlock and Watson stared at where the dog was a little bit longer, then turned to each other with worried expressions.

Not sure what to do about the dog, they refocused on the Manor, and when they approached the door, Sherlock rang the doorbell. Though they were outside, they could hear the bell clearly. It was deep, and loud, like a church bell ringing from the tower. The tones of the bell made Sherlock and Watson look at one another in a worried way.

Eventually, the sound of the bell subsided, and silence filled the area. No one answered the door. Sherlock moved towards the doorbell but Watson stopped him.

"No! I'm not hearing that again," he noted firmly.

"It's a doorbell, Watson," teased Sherlock.

"Yes, one that creeps me out, just like the rest of this town. If you want to persist, knock."

Sherlock rolled his eyes, but gave in to Watson's request. He knocked on the door in a way to ensure that it was heard, as well as not be mistaken for a random object hitting the door. While he waited, Sherlock turned and examined the area, a curious look grew on his face, but he snapped out of it when the door handle turned.

The door slowly opened, but not by much, just enough for a lone eye to peer through it and observe who was knocking at the door.

"This is not a tourist destination," said a low, grim voice.

"We're not tourists," said Sherlock, stepping forward to ensure the eye was fixed on him, "we're investigators, Mr. Baskerville. There are some very odd things going on in your town, and we believe you're a part of it. We wish to ask you some questions."

A stare down began between the two, neither side willing to give an inch and show weakness. But, soon, a laugh filled the area, it was coming from Baskerville. He shut the door, and a latch could be heard. After that, the door opened, and Baskerville could be seen in full.

The first thing Sherlock noticed was his face, while it was young in shape and form, it had an experienced expression on it, one that made him look significantly older than he was. Moving on, he noticed his clothes were both fashionable and regal looking. There wasn't a stain nor crease on them. His posture was straight and true. He stood with authority, and gazed at them as if he was their superior, which in a way, he was.

He observed the two for a few moments then motioned them in, "Might as well come in if you're going to ask questions."

Baskerville left the doorway. Sherlock and Watson turned to one another and nodded before entering. Once inside, it became clear just how elegant the household was. It was pristine in its upkeep. Everything was spotless, and made to look like a treasure unto itself. The materials that made the house were a mix of wood and stone, but refined in a way so that they wouldn't crumble or degrade.

Watson was really taken aback by the look of the place, but Sherlock merely scanned around for clues. Baskerville watched them with a wry smile, "Impressive, isn't it? This is one of the legacies of my family."

"It is...an impressive legacy," acknowledged Watson, still in awe.

"Yes, quaint," added Sherlock, briskly. "Now, about those questions?"

Baskerville laughed this time, "Ah, yes. You think I'm involved in something going on in town?"

"Well, it is your town. Isn't that one of the other legacies of your family?"

"Yes. One that's bore much fruit."

"Truly, including the fruit of kidnapping and death?"

"I don't find that funny."

Sherlock chuckled, which unnerved Baskerville. Sherlock though took a step closer, "We're here because a man disappeared a few days ago, he was last seen in this town, with his sister. Your police said they couldn't find him, I don't believe them. Then, we were told that despite your desire for privacy, you have people up here often. Soon after that, someone goes missing. That's a very odd coincidence. Wouldn't you agree, Mr. Baskerville?"

Their staring contest began once again, each gaze boring into the others as if trying to read each others' minds. Again, Baskerville was the first to break, and again, it was with a smile, "Like you said, an odd coincidence. But not proof of anything. Also, like you said, this is basically my town. An...inheritance you might say. As such, the leaders of this town meet me with to discuss things that are going on. Hardly a crime."

"Indeed."

They again stared at each other, Watson watched this anxiously, not sure of what to do. But, an idea soon popped into his head, "Mr. Baskerville, do you live here alone? I ask because the place is spotless, that must take a lot of work to keep it clean all by yourself."

Baskerville broke his contest with Sherlock and walked over to Watson, "Good observation. While I did inherit quite a bit from my family, I unfortunately got the bad bits as well. My father died when he was only 60, as did his father. The remaining members of my family are all gone as well. To ensure I could survive should I be left alone, my father taught me how to take care of myself, and this mansion, all on my own. It helps me pass the time."

"That's incredible discipline, sir."

"Good to be appreciated in that regard," he said with an honest smile. "Now, if you are done with your questions, I would ask you to leave."

Sherlock took one last look around, "We shall. One last question though. Do you have a dog?"

"No. I would think the cleanness of the household would prove that. A dog would make a rather big mess."

"That they would. That's we don't have one in our flat. Come Watson."

"Right," Watson said, before giving a small bow to Baskerville and leaving.

Baskerville watched them exit, then head down the path for a while before closing the door.

Sherlock and Watson continued to walk away for a few seconds, but once the door closed Watson turned back, then looked at Sherlock, "Well?"

"He's lying," he noted with a grimace.

"Of course he's lying! But about what?"

"Several things. First off, he most certainly has a dog. There were small clues that proved that. There was a claw mark on the leg of the table I was nearby. Also, though disguised, I detected a whiff of dog hair."

Watson scoffed, "That could've been from us! There are dogs everywhere in this town!"

He continued on, only to realize Sherlock wasn't with him. Watson turned around to see Sherlock gazing at him, shaking his head in mock disappointment. Watson rolled his eyes at this, "Alright! Alright! He has a dog, forgive me for mocking your nose."

Sherlock chuckled at his frustration, "You're forgiven. The question now is, why did he lie about that? As you said, everyone has a dog, so why lie about that specifically?"

"Breaks the illusion of wanting to be alone?"

"Very outside the box, perception is reality after all. It's possible, but it doesn't feel right. Ok, let's head back to town. We need to..."

Sherlock stopped suddenly and looked out towards the nearby hillside. When Watson noticed this, he turned to where Sherlock was looking, and standing on a nearby rock was the Belgian Malinois from before. Unlike before though, it wasn't giving a look of examination, but rather, an intense look, a determined one.

"Why is it staring at us like that?" Watson asked.

"I'm not sure, but I doubt it's a coincidence that it's back," noted Sherlock, eyes glued to the dog.

Suddenly, and surprisingly, the dog made a motion with his head, as if to say to follow him. Both Sherlock and Watson were stunned by this, especially when the dog did it a few more times before turning and heading up a hill and turning back to them.

Watson was still stunned, but managed to speak out, "Did that dog just tell us to follow him?"

"He did," replied Sherlock with a smile, very intrigued at the turn of events, "let's accept the invitation."

Carefully, yet with haste, they followed the dog. First to the hill it was on, and then, down it and towards the nearby forest. They exchanged a look of concern as they got closer to it, but they felt they had to follow.

The dog led them right to the edge of the forest before it disappeared from their view. Despite the sun being out still, the trees in the forest were so packed together that light didn't pass through them.

Watson tried to make out where the dog went, "Where did it go?"

"Hmm...do you have you have a flashlight app on your phone?" asked Sherlock.

"You don't?"

"Just shut up and turn it on."

With a smile, Watson pulled out his phone and clicked on an app. Once the light was on, he pointed it towards the trees. As he did, a small opening was revealed, "Oh, maybe he went through there."

"More than likely. Let's go. Slowly though, something feels off about this."

"Which part? The dog leading us to a forest of potential death? Or the fact that the dog seems as smart as us?"

"Both, now lead the way."

Watson grunted but did so, taking each step slowly as the forest closed in around them. The area was already quiet, but as they entered the forest, it seemed to get even quieter. Only their footsteps made a noise. Their expressions grew more sour with each step, but they continued onward.

Suddenly, as Watson was panning the area with his light, a flash of color appeared, "Sherlock! Look."

Sherlock moved to get a better viewpoint, and in front of them was the Belgian Malinois, but this time, it wasn't alone. For in front of it was a dead body. Even more curious, the dog seemed sad as it looked down at it.

"It led us to a body?"

"Yes, but I'm curious as to why," noted Sherlock.

He put his hands up to show he was no threat, and slowly he approached the body. Watson hesitated at first, but when the dog didn't move, he joined him.

The body was decaying, and its skin and clothes were ragged and torn. Making sure to keep an eye on the dog, Sherlock and Watson made to examine it.

"What can you tell me, Watson?"

"Uh, let's see. Numerous slash marks, definitely male, my word, his skin is eviscerated, look at it!"

"I'm looking, Watson, believe me. Focus. What do you see?"

"Sorry, sorry. Decay has set in, hard to say how the forest has affected the rate but I'd guess...he's been dead three or four days."

Sherlock sighed heavily, "Who do we know that's been missing that amount of time?"

Watson shook his head sadly, "Kenny. Dee is going to be devastated."

"Yes, she will, but, she can find solace in knowing the why, the how, and the who. Let's start with how."

"Right."

More determined, Watson examined the body with his flashlight. His eyes moved from one wound to another attempting to figure out what had happened to Kenny. Sherlock waited patiently, occasionally eyeing the dog to see if it had changed its position or expression.

Watson turned to Sherlock once he was done, his face frightened, "Sherlock, we have a problem."

"What? Can't tell the cause of death?"

"Oh, that was easy, but the truth is unnerving. I see no fewer than four different sized claw marks on his body. There's also at least three different sets of teeth marks. Including this bite on the neck that probably killed him. There's only one explanation, he was attacked by a pack of wild dogs."

"While not comforting, it does make sense. There are wild dogs in this forest, we've been told that. And our 'guide' here proved it."

"Sherlock, you don't get it," he said frustrated, "this attack? It was coordinated! These dogs worked together to kill him! Different breeds! That's rare outside of wolf packs. It just doesn't happen."

"Huh," said Sherlock strumming his chin, "so why did it happen here? Why did they feel they needed to attack him? Kill him?"

"Here's another question, what was he doing here? Remember what Dee said? Kenny went missing when he went looking for a landmark. There's no landmarks in this forest! Even if there was, he would've told her that he was going to the forest, right?"

"Given their relationship, very likely. So, why was he here, and why did the dogs attack him in this spot?"

As if to answer that question, the dog moved over a few feet, and pointed his head to the ground. Sherlock motioned Watson to light up the area, and the two observed disturbed ground and leaves.

"Oh, you dragged him here, didn't you? Why?"

Sherlock gazed at the dog, who gazed back before turning and pointing to another section of the forest. This intrigued Sherlock.

"Ok, yes, he was further from this spot. A place that no one would find him. You wanted to make sure he was found."

"Please stop," begged Watson, getting close to a frenzied state, "you can't speak dog, even you aren't that smart."

"It's not about that, it's observation. The ground is disturbed in a wide area, the dog couldn't make that mark. Also, I bet if we looked at the back of Kenny's sweatshirt..."

He carefully moved Kenny, and smiled when he saw scrape marks and dirt covering the back of the shirt.

"There you go, he was dragged, by that dog. He wanted us to find the body."

"And how would he know someone was looking for him?"

Sherlock turned to the dog, then smiled, "Dee. She said a dog walked through town with Kenny's scarf, and when she called out to it, the dog dropped off the scarf and ran away."

"So this is that dog? This is insane."

"Quite possibly, but it's the only thing that makes sense. Ok boy, you showed us the body, now, where did--"

He froze as the dog suddenly started looking around, its expression became one of fear.

"That can't be good."

Sure enough, the dog reared around, lowered itself into an aggressive posture and growled loudly. Sherlock and Watson looked into the darkness of the forest. Soon, bright lights appeared, pairs of them. They were followed by growls of a different nature, and from the darkness emerged many different wild dogs. Their eyes were glowing, and they all were bearing their teeth.

Watson quickly pulled out his pistol, and pointed it at each of the dogs in kind, unsure of which to shoot first, "Sherlock? What do we do?"

"Run," he said softly.

"What?"

"Run!"

Sherlock bolted, and Watson followed, the Malinois though stayed behind and blocked the dogs from chasing after the two. The wild dogs converged on it, but it didn't back down. Instead, it howled loudly before pouncing on them and attacking.

Now a good distance away from the forest, and realizing they weren't being followed, Sherlock and Watson turned back to the forest. Sherlock's expression was intense, as if what happened was a personal sleight against him.

Watson though was more sorrowful, "I feel bad, leaving that dog behind."

"As do I, but it intended to stay, that's why it went into that pose instead of joining us in running. It probably saved our lives. But don't mourn for it, Watson, something tells me we'll see it again."

"It was five-on-one Sherlock, and some of those wild dogs were bigger than it."

"Don't...mourn. Trust me on this."

He gave a knowing smile, which made Watson roll his eyes, "Alright, alright. So what now?"

"Let's head back to the inn. There's much we need to discuss, and I don't want to do it in the open. Come."

Not waiting for a reply, Sherlock marched off. Watson took one last look at the forest before pocketing his gun and following him.

It took them a little while, but they soon returned to the inn, and went straight for their rooms. Sherlock again watched the eyes of the people of the town as they walked through it, and noticed that they were very intense in their glares at them. This caused him to think quietly to himself for some time once they were safe in their room.

Watson took this time to clean himself up. As he washed his hands, he noticed that they were shaking. Whether it was from the sight of the dogs, the fact that they barely escaped being mauled by them, or the sight of Kenny, he was rattled. He took a moment and did several deep breaths until the shaking stopped. Watson finished with his cleaning before joining Sherlock.

"Think of anything yet?" Watson asked when he noticed Sherlock was still in his thinking pose.

"Too many questions," Sherlock replied bluntly.

"True, shall I ask the obvious one then?"

"By all means."

"Did we really see the eyes of those wild dogs glow?"

The question caused Sherlock to move into a different thinking pose, which made Watson chuckle. He remained in the pose for a few seconds before turning to Watson, "Yes, we did. Your apps' light didn't have enough power to make their eyes glow."

"Not to mention we couldn't see their pupils."

"Good observation. So, question, what could make a dogs eyes glow?"

"Naturally, or unnaturally?" posed Watson.

"Another good question. If those dogs are truly wild, then there's no way they'd let humans do anything to them. However, there is another option, one that is tied to the history of this town..."

"The military facility."

Sherlock tapped his nose to show Watson was on the mark, "Dogs are viable test subjects, and who's to say the dogs they experimented on didn't escape into the forest while the building burnt down? If they did experiment on them, and they continued to breed, the genes would've passed down."

"Possible, but that raises another question. Why would the military want to make glowing eyes for dogs?"

"To scare the crap out of people, duh."

He looked to Watson, who looked back with a serious expression. The two then broke into laughter. Watson nodded his head as he went to his bed and sat on it, "Well played. I'm sure the military would do that for the record."

"Oh, no doubt. Psychological warfare is huge. Imagine an army of 'demon dogs' bursting into an enemy camp. The hysteria would be very enticing for them. But no, that's not the answer. Where are the remains of the facility? In proximity to where we are?"

Watson thought about it, then pulled out his phone and researched it. He pulled up a map and showed it to Sherlock, "About a mile outside the city, opposite direction of the manor."

Sherlock looked at the map with great curiosity, even using his finger to draw connections only he could see, "Interesting. Shall we go visit?"

"Is that an option?"

"I don't know, is it a restricted area?"

Again, Watson went to his phone and typed on it. After a few moments he made a noise of surprise, "No, it's not. They cleared it out and opened it up to the public a few years back. It was...huh..."

"What, what?"

"...an initiative, one started by Rudolph Baskerville, in order to, "bring the fullness of the area back to life and to its people.""

Watson showed the article to Sherlock, who smiled widely at this, "Very interesting. Let's go to the facility."

"I'm bringing my gun."

"As you should, and you have my blessing to carry it throughout the rest of this case. I know we'll need it."

With a knowing nod to the other, they rose up and made their way out of their room.

Chapter Five: Hidden Meaning

Sherlock and Watson again made their way through the town. Again, they couldn't help but notice that the townspeople were staring at them. Watson became uneasy at all the glares, but Sherlock, he glared right back at them, showing no hesitation or fear in regards to their looks. He honestly tried to meet every single pair of eyes that sent a glare their way.

Once on the outskirts, Sherlock recommended they pause to ensure they weren't being followed. A few minutes passed, and no one came around where they were, so they progressed.

They trekked a beaten path through a nearby hillside, and followed it for a while. As they did, Watson pulled out his phone and typed on it. Sherlock meanwhile kept his gaze vigilant, making sure that nothing escaped his notice, even spinning around at times to ensure that no one from the town had figured out where they were going and decided to follow.

Twenty minutes passed, and they reached the end of the path. Both Sherlock and Watson gazed curiously at what was in front of them.

It was the remains of a facility, but one that had long since been gone and deconstructed. The only thing that seemed to remain was the floor of the building, which was made of marble and certain other materials. The terrain around the building had tried to grow into it, and over it, with some success. If you didn't know what it was, you might have suspected it was a failed building, not one that burned down.

"I'm at amazed at nature at times," noted Watson with a small smile, "give it enough time, and it will envelope just about anything put upon it."

"True, but I'd admire more the construction of man at this juncture," mused Sherlock.

"How so?"

"Look! Yes, nature has overtaken much of what's left, but not all. There's still plenty of floor patches that aren't touched by grass or weeds. It's been over thirty years since it burned down, and it's still not overtaken."

"Huh, good point. That seems odd though, but I don't know why."

"It'll come to you I'm sure. Now, what do we know about the experiments that went on here?"

Watson pulled out his phone again, and scrolled the screen with his finger for a bit, "Ah, here it is. The Penzington Institute was a military-based science station--"

Sherlock laughed loudly, "That's an oxymoron."

"Can I continue?"

"Yes, sorry."

"Military-based science station dedicated to the research of plant and animal life within the native area where humanity had not spread."

"If they're doing what we think they were doing...that's somewhat accurate."

"There's more. Grants and funding given to the science station were attributed to the research of plant-based medicine and health enhancements."

"Drugs, steroids, and super serums."

"Possibly. Bit ironic if you think about it, you know, this happening in the 80's."

Sherlock laughed again, but this time in an ironic way, "Oh Watson, it started long before then. I have proof."

With a scoff, Watson shook his head and made to chastise Sherlock, but paused when he saw the serious expression upon his face, "You're serious?"

"Oh yes. Cold case I did once. Tragic results for those involved. Another story for another time."

Leaving Watson to wonder what he meant, Sherlock stepped onto the floor of the former institute. He looked for clues of any kind to try and make sense of what was really going on there. Yet, with just a floor, one weathered by time and nature, there wasn't much to gather.

Frustrated, he started to pace, which made Watson chuckle, Sherlock glared at him when he did "Don't!"

Watson put his hands up in mock surrender, "I didn't say a word."

"You didn't have to. If I wanted to criticize my habits I'd call Mycroft...oh...there's an idea."

"You want to call Mycroft to criticize you?"

Sherlock whipped out his phone and dialed a number quickly, "No, but I do want to call Mycroft. He loves finding old military secrets."

"Because he likes history?"

"Ha! No. Because he can use them against people if done correctly. This one time he...brother! Hello. Time to cash in one of those favors you owe me."

His eyes narrowed as Mycroft spoke, "Lying doesn't become you, brother. You owe me five favors...yes, five!

London, France, that time in Denmark, that other time in Denmark and the Wind Fish incident! Five!"

He let his brother speak again, and after a bit he gave a motion of acceptance, "You're right, it's three. I apologize. I had forgotten about the Majin Files and the Runner incident."

Watson grunted, "I haven't."

"Shush, Watson. Anyway, you can go from three to two right now. I need to know what the Penzington Institute was researching back in the 80's. It's the one that burned down near the town of Baskerville."

Sherlock's eyebrow raised after a response from his brother, "Oh? You've been keeping an eye on the town? Interesting. We're here on a case, a man was murdered by wild dogs and we want to see if the military was inadvertently involved via their experiments."

He paused again, and made an over-the-top gaping at a statement from Mycroft, "Yes...it's a...dog eat dog world out there..."

"Tell me he didn't actually say that," begged Watson, offended.

Sherlock nodded and waited for Mycroft to speak again. A minute passed by with nothing, but then, he returned, "Yes, brother, I'm still here. What did you find? ...nothing related to dogs? You're sure? Oh, nothing that clearly states dogs, that is different. Hmm...let me think."

Lowering his phone, he turned to face the facility floor. He observed the layout and walked it for a bit, then saw something odd. He touched the floor with his fingertips, then put his cell back to his ear, "Brother, how many floors did this building have?"

"What does that matter?" asked Watson, but was waved down by Sherlock.

"Three? Was one of them a basement? Excellent! Alright, I'll be in touch. Keep your phone nearby, I'm certain I'm going to need your help again. ...what? Yes, it'll count as another favor. Goodbye, brother."

With a noise of disapproval Sherlock hung up and put his phone away. Watson came over and joined him, "Get what you need?"

"Look at the floor, what do you see?"

Watson walked in a circle for a bit, observing as much of the floor as he could see. When done, he shrugged, "A floor being overgrown by nature."

"Close. A floor mostly being overgrown by nature. Look at this spot here. Notice how there isn't a single blade of grass or weed in this area from the ground up?"

"Huh, you're right. What does it mean though?"

"It means..."

Sherlock began tapping on the floor, waiting to hear what he needed to. Eventually, a hollow sound came from a spot. He smiled, and felt around the spot until his hands pushed down on an area which contained a spring mechanism under a part of the floor. After he pushed it down and released it, the floor panel sprang up, revealing a staircase underneath it.

"Wow," said Watson amazed.

"Wow indeed. A hidden basement, let's see what's inside. Give me your phone, I want to use the flashlight."

Watson turned on the app and gave it to Sherlock, who immediately used it to observe the staircase. He smiled as he did, "Good, it's stone, I'm grateful. "

"Because if it was wood it would've likely rotted by now?"

"Precisely, and that would've been risky to step on. But the stone should be fine. Let's go."

Confident, but still careful, Sherlock led the way down the stairs. He did his best to shine the light on everything in his immediate area to ensure they didn't bump into something or trigger an old security system.

Once they hit the basement floor, the two looked around where they could. They were in a lab of some kind, and its age showed. There were outdated desks and computers scattered throughout. Dust was over pretty much everything, as well as rust on the metal parts. Upon further observation though, there were clear signs of things being removed from the room. Certain desk drawers were open and had nothing within them, mainframes for the computers had little to no innards.

As he saw this, Watson scratched his head in confusion, "Was someone here recently?"

"No, you're thinking short-term because of what we read about Baskerville cleaning this place up," noted Sherlock as he continued to look around. "When the facility burned down, it clearly destroyed the floors above. As you can see here, this floor was mostly untouched by the fire.

To avoid suspicion of their experiments, as well as get rid of most of the evidence, the military likely took what they needed and ran."

"Makes sense. So if all the evidence is gone, why are we here? What can we hope to find?"

Sherlock made to respond, but stopped and gazed at something in front of him.

His silence got Watson's attention, "Sherlock?"

"Found."

"What?"

"Not hoping to find...found."

He turned to his partner and pointed. Watson came closer, and his eyes went wide. For in front of them was a dog cage. It was old, and very bent out of shape. But it had a label just under it that read, "Fido."

Watson just stood there gaping at the cage, "You've got to be kidding me."

"Fido is a great name for a dog."

"No! I meant they really did experiment on dogs."

"I told you they make great test subjects."

"Shut up, Sherlock. I'm serious."

"So was I."

He glared at Sherlock, who put his hands up in surrender and took a step back. Composing himself, Watson stepped closer to the cage and examined it. After a few seconds he sighed in relief.

This got Sherlock's attention, "What?"

"Well, the cage is bent in certain places. Made me wonder what caused it. Thankfully, based on where the metal is bent, it was done from the outside, not the inside," he noted as he pointed out the bent areas.

"Meaning?"

"Meaning that they didn't create a super soldier dog! Or a heightened strength feral one. The dog didn't cause this damage. There might have been an accident or something that caused it."

"Likely the chaos from the fire shook things loose."

"Possible. So, we found a dog cage, what now?"

Sherlock pondered this for a while, then used the phone to illuminate the room again, "Let's keep looking, I think there's something here still. Just don't know what."

Not waiting for Watson, he began to search the room again, looking high and low for any clue that might help him crack the case. Watson shook his head but followed Sherlock around the room. Despite it being cleared of files and computer data, there was still a lot there.

For as Sherlock shined a light on certain areas, a lot of chemistry equipment was found. Test tubes, beakers, burners, filtration units, chemical mixers, and more. All indicating some high-level experiments.

"What were they trying to do to that dog?" asked Watson as he saw all of this, "I may not be able to guess what chemicals were in this lab, but there was something big going on here."

"No doubt," acknowledged Sherlock grimly, "knowing the military, it was nothing good."

"Bet Mycroft would love to lead an institute like this."

"Actually, Mycroft is against experimenting on animals, of any kind."

"Really?"

"Oh yes, he finds it cruel. As he told me once, why use animals when you can use people instead?"

Watson's jaw dropped at the statement, and Sherlock gave no indication to whether he was joking or not. Rather, he kept looking around the lab. After shaking off the shock, Watson rejoined him.

They eventually made their way to a series of filing cabinets. All of them had drawers open to various extents, and all of them were empty as well. Sherlock hissed in aggravation at the lack of any clues, and lowered the hand with the phone in it as he rubbed his forehead with the other. As he did though, Watson saw something.

"Sherlock! There's something behind this cabinet."

Watson kneeled down and pointed to something sticking out behind the far right cabinet. Sherlock smiled when he saw it.

He gave the phone back to Watson, "Keep it pointed at that."

Watson did so, and Sherlock got a good position and slowly moved the cabinet forward. Once he had enough space he reached down and grabbed the item.

Once he got a good luck at it, Sherlock laughed loudly, "What are the odds?"

"What? What is it?" Watson asked eagerly.

He flipped the paper around for Watson to see, "This, Watson, is a bio file...on Fido."

"Great, because we totally need to know to more about the dog that was experimented on!"

"Every piece of information helps, Watson, you know that. Alright, let's see here."

Sherlock turned the page back around so he could read, then quickly read over every line. He mouthed them as he did so, but didn't read them aloud so Watson could hear. Watson rolled his eyes and cleared his throat loudly. When Sherlock looked up and saw his expression he recoiled slightly.

"Sorry, habit."

"I know, just give me the gist of it."

"Basically, Fido was a perfectly normal dog undergoing something called Project EL. There's a smudge over certain sections, I think it's early test results, probably health related. After that...oh my."

"What? What does it say?"

Sherlock's expression hardened as he looked at Watson, "That Fido was donated to the institute by Sir Magnus Baskerville. The father of Rudolph Baskerville."

Watson whistled at this piece of news, "That can't be a coincidence."

"No, it cannot."

With new passion, Sherlock poured over the document some more, and his eyes grew more angry with each line he read. Once done, he folded the paper and put it into an interior pocket of his jacket.

"We need to go."

"Why? Where?" asked as began to follow Sherlock, who was heading for the staircase.

"Baskerville Manor! Sir Rudolph has a lot of explaining to do."

With that, Sherlock raced up the stairs, Watson in tow. Once at the top, Sherlock pushed the floor panel back down, concealing the lab once more. He motioned for Watson to follow, and ran off towards the town.

Sherlock ran as quickly as he could, and Watson was able to keep up with him despite the height difference between them. During a section of running on a flat plain, Watson noticed Sherlock's face was very pained, and he didn't know why.

"What aren't you telling me?" he shouted as they ran.

"I know why Baskerville lied about not having a dog!" he shouted back.

"Why did he?"

"Trust me, you're better off not knowing right now."

"That's hardly reassuring."

"Let's just say if you knew, you might not want to return to the town. Ignorance is bliss, at least for a little while longer."

This statement made Watson angry, "Are you calling me a coward?"

"No, I'm calling you smart. You're afraid of the town, and if you knew what that paper said, and what I put together in my head, you'd be terrified."

"And you're not?"

"Yeah, I am," he said with a nervous laugh, "but we have to do this."

They continued to run, the town getting closer as they did. Watson cycled through many emotions as he thought about what Sherlock said, before finally going stone-faced and noting, "I hate you."

"I know. Doubt that's about to change."

Sherlock gave a wry smile to Watson, who scoffed and gave one back. Now on the same page, they focused back on getting to the town. Once they were within a hundred feet of it they slowed down, and made sure they didn't look too suspicious as they re-entered.

Sherlock pulled out his phone once they made it onto the entry street, "I might need to call Mycroft for backup. This could get ugly. But should I do it now or later? It could spook the locals to see armed soldiers in their town..."

While he pondered what to do, Watson looked around the street nervously. With each rotation, his expression grew more and more fearful, "Sherlock?"

"Just a second, Watson. Maybe I could have them meet me at the manor...that could limit the unease. But if they fly in, that would raise a lot of suspicion as well."

"Sherlock..."

"One second! Better safe than sorry, I can't risk--"

"SHERLOCK!" Watson roared.

"What?" he roared back.

"Look around! Where is everyone?!?"

Confused, Sherlock span around to observe the street they were on. Sure enough, it was empty, not a soul in sight. This made Sherlock very uneasy.

"What in the world...? Come on, let's check another main street."

Running once more, they made their way down one street, and then to another, each one though was empty, as if the whole town was evacuated while they were away.

They eventually made their way to the main street of the town, and even that was empty. Both Sherlock and Watson looked into the windows of stores and nearby houses, but no one could be found.

All of the denizens of Baskerville were missing.

Face full of fear, Watson turned to Sherlock, "What does this mean?"

Sherlock sighed heavily before turning to his friend, "We're screwed."

Chapter Six: Prey

Being mindful of their surroundings, Sherlock and Watson rushed to the inn. They made sure that once they were inside that nothing was waiting to surprise them, but no one was in the inn, not even at the front desk.

"What the heck?" asked Watson as he looked around, "This makes no sense."

"Actually, it does," lamented Sherlock, "come on, we need to grab some things."

With a nod, Watson followed Sherlock to their room. They again checked for any surprises, but again, no one was there. The two went for their bags, and went to some special pockets within them to get some items. Watson grabbed a few extra magazine clips and put them on his person.

Sherlock noticed this and shook his head, "How many did you bring?"

"I'm scared of this town, remember?" teased Watson.

"Well played."

Sherlock pulled out some small sealed pouches and put them on his person in various places. Once set, they made to leave, but Watson stopped Sherlock, "Wait, where are we going?"

"I told you, Baskerville Manor."

"Still?"

"As ironic as it may sound, it's the only safe place right now."

Watson reached behind him, "Should I have my gun out?"

Sherlock thought about it, then shook his head, "No, not yet. Let's play this out. Besides, if there is a logical explanation for all of this, aside from the one I'm thinking, we don't want to cause an incident."

"Alright. Let's go."

Cautiously, they made their way into the hallway, then to the front area, then with a careful glance to ensure there were no surprises, they went onto the street, and ran towards the edge of town. As they did, they repeatedly looked around to see if there was anyone around, but there wasn't.

As they made it down the last road, an item bounced towards them from a nearby alley. Sherlock's eyes went wide as he saw it, "Flash bang!"

Before they could stop and dodge, the flash bang exploded, and both Sherlock and Watson were thrown backwards, hitting the ground hard. Watson tried to see what was going on, but all he could make out were a pair of silhouettes standing over them, when he tried to extend a hand for help, one of the silhouettes made a motion towards his head, and he blacked out.

Sometime later, Sherlock awoke. The moment he had his wits about he immediately tried to ascertain everything that was going on. He found himself tied to a chair, both his arms and legs bound, making it impossible to move too much.

He struggled for a few seconds to see just how bound he was, when it was clear he wasn't going to get any leverage he stopped. Sherlock closed his eyes and took a deep breath, then another. He could feel his heartbeat slow. Once he was content with his state of mind he opened his eyes again and began to observe the room.

It didn't take long for a smile to grow on his face, then a laugh to follow. He quieted it though and looked around again, "Where are you Rudolph? Is this any way to treat a guest?"

"Depends on the guest," said a voice.

Sherlock turned, and from a nearby doorway came Rudolph Baskerville, his expression smug. He walked towards Sherlock, who feigned sadness at his arrival, "I'm sorry I can't get up to shake your hand, but I'm currently tied to a chair."

"I'll manage."

"I'm sure you will. Care to tell me why I'm here?

"I think you know, you're too nosy for your own good."

"I like to solve mysteries, sue me."

It was Rudolph who laughed this time, "Oh, I think I can come up with worse things to do to you. But first, let us talk. How much do you know?

"Enough to put you and most this town behind bars."

Again, Rudolph laughed, but this time, he went and got another chair and placed it in front of Sherlock before sitting in it, "Do tell."

Sherlock smiled, and slowly maneuvered his hands so that they touched one of his arms, "Where should I start?

The murders? The dogs? The military? There's so much to talk about, so little time."

"I think we'll make time," Baskerville said menacingly. "How about the dogs? I told you I didn't have one, yet you seem to not believe that. What made you dig deeper into that?"

"Your house isn't as clean as you might think, there are scents that belong to dogs, and scratches on your furniture too. But the real tip was from the military facility. Inside front pocket in my jacket. Go ahead, I won't bite."

With a smile, Sherlock taunted Baskerville to do so. Baskerville bought in, and pulled the paper out, "Let's see, Fido...? I haven't heard that name in a long time. Donated to the military by my father...personally selected...ah...I see."

"Personally selected from his dog ranch," finished Sherlock with satisfaction. "Watson and I never saw the back of the house, and the train enters and leaves in a direction that the back isn't seen. I was wondering where all the dogs came and went to, and now I know. You don't a single dog, you own a whole pack!"

"No crime in that."

"It is when you sick them on people!"

"And why would I do that?"

For the first time in the conversation, uncertainty grew on Sherlock's face, "I don't know. I first thought you were a depraved mind, but I'm not sure if that's the case. Whatever your motivations are, they aren't pure. Killing like this, so viciously, through your own dogs? It doesn't matter why you do it, you do it."

Baskerville made a noise of disgust and rolled his eyes, "Such platitudes, right and wrong. You don't even have a motive for me doing such things! Yet, you're so sure it's me."

"Oh, it's you. You're a Baskerville, you run this town. You give an order, they follow. Such as letting you know when a new tourist is in town. After all, you fill the inn with your lackeys."

"How so?" asked Baskerville with mock surprise.

"It wasn't obvious, to be fair. But certain things didn't add up. How could an inn in a remote town, one with such a dangerous history only have one room open? Yes, it made sense that the previous tourists, one of which you killed, had to leave, but no one else? Then, when you "evacuated" the town, that included the inn people. There was no one there. A tourist wouldn't know what to do when the signal came down from above. They would've been just like me and Watson..."

Suddenly afraid, Sherlock looked around, expression growing more fearful and agitated with each passing second, "Where is Watson?!?"

Baskerville watched as Sherlock continued to look around, then he leaned in and smiled, "You're smart. Guess."

Far away, in the forest just outside Baskerville, Watson laid on the ground, face buried in leaves and dirt. With a groan, he started to stir. His body ached still from the attack, especially his head. He felt his forehead and recoiled when he felt a bump on it.

"Ow," Watson said lowly.

Still struggling, but managing to gather his strength, he made it to his feet. Watson's eyes took a while to take to the lighting of the area, but they eventually did so.

"What the...? Where am I?

He looked around, and his eyes went wide when he noticed some familiar things. Mainly, the kinds of trees that surrounded him.

"Oh no, I'm in the forest...which means..."

Watson's breathing quickened, and he went into a state of panic. Looking around feverishly, expecting an attack from any and all directions. But, not unlike what

Sherlock did in his predicament, he calmed himself down. Taking deep breathes and regaining his focus.

"Calm down, Watson," he told himself. "If you panic, you make mistakes. Deep breaths, just like they taught you in med school. Ok, I'm in a forest with known hostiles, mainly wild dogs. I need protection...oh!"

He reached behind his back, and laughed when he saw that his gun was still on him. Watson checked the ammo, and sure enough, it was all there. As were the extra clips on his person.

"Ha! Whoever knocked me out didn't search me. Lucky break. One of the few I'm going to get. Ok, I can't see the sun or any clouds because of the canopy. Let's search for some moss and head south, that'll lead me towards town. Hopefully anyway."

Cocking his gun, Watson slowly moved through the forest, making sure to keep his head on a swivel for any threats. As he did though, pairs of eyes began to shine through the dark areas of the forest.

Back at the manor, Sherlock bared his teeth at his "host", "If he gets harmed you won't have to fear the police, I'll rip you limb from limb."

"I'm so scared," Baskerville mocked. "I wouldn't worry about your friend. After he's gone, you'll be next. I just wanted to make sure I knew what you had on me before I fed you to the dogs. You have nothing but circumstantial evidence and conjecture and a military paper that says I have a lot of dogs. And with you gone, not even your word can be used against me."

"Now it is you who underestimate me, sir. I have more than you realize."

"Oh? How so?"

"Simple, I'm actually quite used to the effects of flash bang grenades, I test them out on myself whenever I get bored. Watson doesn't like loud noises, so I do it when he's away."

"Your point?" asked Baskerville not amused.

"I saw who knocked us out. Your officer lackeys, Myers and Jay. I knew they were corrupt when we took a peak at your file system. It took me a while, but I figured out your acronym for P.F.H. Perfect. For. Hunt. We have pictures of those files, and before leaving the inn I took a sec to program them to go to a friend of mine in Scotland Yard. He'll get everything we found."

"Miscellaneous documents with random acronyms that make sense only in your mind! And as for Myers and Jay, they won't roll on me, especially since you won't be able to accuse them since you'll...be...dead."

Sherlock smiled widely, which got Baskerville to lean in, for he was curious.

"Seriously? A smile? Is this how you face death?"

"I'll say it again, Baskerville, now it's you who are underestimating me," noted Sherlock still smiling.

"And I'll say it again, how so?"

"Because, I know I'm not going to die, and I'm going to save Watson before he dies. Do you know why? Because I don't go away, I don't stop when a mystery in front of me can be solved, and most importantly of all...

With an even wider smile, he put his hands in front of him for Baskerville to see, there was a small blade in his left hand. Baskerville went from it to the floor where the ropes that bound his hands now lay. He went wide-eyed at this, "What?"

"...I have both my hands free, which means--"

Before finishing, Sherlock sent a right hook at Baskerville, clocking him clean in the jaw, and sending him flying to the ground. Sherlock pulled out another blade from his sleeve and cut his legs free. He then went back to

Baskerville, who was stirring a little, and clocked him again in the head, knocking him out cold.

"I don't know if you can hear me, but next time you kidnap a few people? Search them thoroughly."

Content, Sherlock raced out of the house and towards the forest, he pulled out his phone and dialed a number as he did so, "Come on...come on! Mycroft! It's me. I don't care what you have to do, get as many armed personnel as you can and get to Baskerville as soon as possible! The town is part of a conspiracy killing tourists! ...no I'm not joking! Rudolph Baskerville confessed it like a good evil villain should! They have Watson! I'm going after him but I don't know if we'll make it out. You need to get here, now! Thank you! I'm leaving my phone outside the forest that's right by the town, track it, then come and find us. Be combat ready, there are dogs trained to kill humans in the forest. As ironic as it sounds, I don't want you to be a victim, brother."

Sherlock reached the forest, and stood in front of the path he and Watson were at before, "I have to go. We may have an hour, maybe less. Get here, brother, I really do need you."

He closed the phone, and hid it in some nearby leaves where no one would see it. With a deep breath he calmed himself, then rushed in.

Deep into the forest, Watson continued his trek. He moved as carefully as he could while maintaining a good pace. His gun was still in his hand, ready to fire at a moments' notice. With each step, Watson felt the tension within him mount. Multiple times he had to stop and take a calming breath to try and force himself to a calmer state, but it only helped in small ways.

Focused and calm enough to continue, he again made strides towards escape. But just minutes after starting again, he stopped. This time though, it was because a sound reached his ears. It started look, like a hum, but as it grew, it turned into a growl. Knowing what it meant, Watson reared around to try and locate the source of the noise. It didn't take long though, for a pair of glowing eyes appeared from a dark spot within two trees.

Soon, a dog emerged from the darkness, it was a Doberman. It bared its teeth at Watson, slowly approaching him with clear malice.

Watson pointed his gun straight at the dog, "Down, boy. I don't want to hurt you. Don't make me hurt you!"

Whether the dog understood or not, it didn't matter, once within striking distance, the dog lunged at Watson. Reacting quickly, Watson fired the gun, and a bullet hit the dog right in the head, causing it to fall to the ground dead.

Shaken, Watson just looked at the dog for a while, then checked to make sure it was dead. When he confirmed it he got visibly upset, and even punched the ground a few times with his free hand in anger over what had happened.

"I'm sorry," he said to the dog, "I'm sorry."

Before he could lament anymore, the sound of rustling filled his ears. Not wanting to take a chance, Watson prepped his gun for another shot then bolted down a nearby path.

Though he kept his eyes forward when he could, he couldn't help but look back and see if anything was chasing him. There wasn't at first, so he kept going. A howling sound made him stop though. It was long and loud, a howl of lament. Watson felt sorrowful, but he also knew what it meant. The dogs had found their fallen, and they would not hold back if they found him. They would get their revenge.

Knowing what was coming, Watson again made his way down the path. He aimed to go down the same direction when possible, but the forest was so thick, he had to diverge at times to at least stay on a path where he could get through within minimal struggle.

While making it down a certain path, a bark filled the area. It was getting closer to him, and increasing in repetition.

"Blast," Watson grimaced as he continued to run at full speed.

Before too long, the dog's bark became much clearer. Without hesitation though, Watson wheeled around, and once the dog came into sight, he shot him down, then proceeded to run once again, not allowing himself to feel bad about killing another one.

As he continued to make his way through the forest, Watson couldn't help but wonder just how deep into the forest he was put in. He knew he was heading south when he started the trek, and he felt that he was still going that way, but with no clues as to how close he was to an exit of any kind, the hope within him started to fade.

This only became amplified when more dogs appeared to try and kill him. Some came within his line of sight, thus allowing him to react quickly and shoot them before they could get to him. Others though were more stealthy, and struck when he was least expecting it. One dog literally blindsided him and tackled him to the ground. It was a Great Dane, and its sheer size and weight allowed it to pin Watson to the ground momentarily.

With his non-gun hand he held the Dane's head back so it couldn't bite him. Then when he got a shot he fired at it. It took a few rounds though before the Dane was put down.

Watson struggled to his feet after this particular attack. Before he could move on though another dog struck at him from behind, taking him to the ground once again. But this time Watson reacted quickly. He backed up, slipping out of his over jacket, then lined up a shot and killed the dog.

As he went to pick up his jacket, he noticed it perfectly covered the dog, saving him from seeing what he did. He decided to leave it be. Watson checked the rounds in his gun, seeing that he only had a few shots left in the clip. He prepped it for another round of fights and went down the nearest path once again.

Every minute that passed made Watson realize that his time was running out. There was no telling how many dogs were in the forest. Given how many dogs there were in Baskerville, it could be many, even a legion. Yet he had only so many bullets. What would run out first? The bullets, or the dogs? He knew the answer, but he didn't want to say it, not even within his own mind.

Trying his best to keep his confidence up, he pressed on, and to his relief, he went a good stretch of time without a dog attack. This allowed him to take a breather and check on his own wounds. To his relief, he only suffered some scratches. One was pretty deep, as it was from the Dane that tackled him to the ground, but he knew it wouldn't kill him. It would just hurt a lot for a while.

Content that he would survive his wounds, he went on his way. His eyes soon caught a new path, which made Watson smile widely. For when he observed the path, it had footprints on it, recent ones. Energy renewed, he bolted down the path to see where it headed. That joy he felt faded though when it led to a clearing still very much in the woods.

Watson sighed heavily and shook his head, "Blast it all. Can't catch a break. I better...better..."

A odd thing caught his eye, and he approached a set of trees on the opposite side of the clearing. Carved into the trees was a phrase, one word per tree, it read, "End of the line."

Understanding what it meant, Watson readied his gun and wheeled around. Sure enough, a pack of dogs slowly emerged from various parts of the clearing, as well as the path. Watson couldn't believe it, the dogs set him up.

"You were guiding me here," he realized, "in case I did make it by you. You put me in a killing field. Clever dogs."

The dogs continued to approach him. Many were different species, different sizes, but all were united in their goal. Kill.

To his own surprise though, Watson smiled, "You may have gotten me, but I'm not going down easily. Come on!"

As if to answer the challenge, two of the dogs lunged at him. Watson reacted quickly though and shot them both down. Another followed suit, a massive Rottweiler, Watson had to unload several bullets into the dog before it would fall, but as he did, his gun clicked loudly. He was out of rounds in the clip.

"Oh crap."

Watson quickly made to reload his gun, but several dogs rushed him as he tried to. Before he could reload, a few jumped at him, forcing him to lunge away. He got back on stable footing as the dogs continued their pursuit. Thinking fast, Watson flipped the gun in position in his hand, and once they were close enough, he smashed them with the butt of his gun.

The dogs still outnumbered him, but he kept his cool, and continued to smack them away as they got close. It didn't work every time though, and he got scratches and bites on his arms and legs because of it. But he refused to give up, and continued to swing away.

After swatting away a particularly aggressive hound, he found himself enough time to change his magazine. Now reloaded, when the dogs charged, he shot them down one by one. Until they were all dead.

The conflict over, at least for the time being, Watson took a moment to catch his breath. The adrenaline wearing off, he started to truly feel the pain from his wounds. He even fell to one knee when it overwhelmed him.

As he looked through the clearing, he couldn't help but be feel horrified by what he had done. He knew it had to be done, but it didn't make him feel any better about killing all these dogs. Something about seeing them dead, and knowing it was by his hand, made him feel sick to his stomach.

He knew he couldn't focus on such thoughts though, he was still in danger, and there could be more dogs out there. He had to get out.

With an effort, he made it back to his feet and limped towards the opening in the clearing. Before he reached it though, another pair of eyes breached the darkness. Watson instinctively raised his gun, and to his horror, another Great Dane emerged. It was even bigger than the one he killed before.

Despite killing all the dogs before, Watson found himself hesitating on this one. As the dog moved towards him, Watson stepped backward. Not knowing what was behind him, he tripped on one of the dead dogs and fell to the ground. The Dane continued towards him, and Watson aimed his gun back at the dog and fired. Once again though, his gun was empty.

"You've got to be kidding me," groaned Watson as he looked at his gun.

A thousand thoughts ran through Watson's head, but none that would help him in this situation. The Great Dane got within striking distance, and lowered itself to strike. With a growl, it lunged towards Watson, who didn't even try to defend himself.

"No!" shouted a voice.

From the treeline, Sherlock emerged, a thick stick in his hands. He slammed the stick into the dog, knocking it immediately into the ground. Sherlock then reared the stick upwards, and like a golfer, swung it into the dogs' side with enough force to send it several feet away from him.

The Dane didn't get up immediately, so Sherlock turned to Watson and extended a hand, "Are you ok?"

Watson couldn't believe Sherlock was here, and after taking the hand to get back on his feet he hugged Sherlock, "Oh my gosh, you're really here."

"Watson...you're hugging me."

"Huh? Oh, right, sorry."

He broke off the hug, and the two went into a slight laughing fit before quickly sobering up. Sherlock took a moment to notice all the dead dogs around him, "You've been busy."

"Yeah, it's been a rough hour. Or, I think it's been that long, I don't know. What about you? Did you have to fight the wild dogs?"

"No, and they're not wild dogs."

"Excuse me?"

"Every single dog here is owned by Rudolph Baskerville. It's been him guiding everything. The dogs, the townspeople, the kidnappings, everything."

Watson cycled through a variety of emotions, trying to comprehend what Sherlock was saying, "But their eyes! They glow!"

Sherlock pointed to Watson to acknowledge the point, "Right, forgot about that. I have an idea for how they did that particular feat."

He got down on one knee and observed one of the dogs Watson killed. Sherlock carefully opened one of its eyes, seeing the glow as it did. He used his free hand touched the eye, then smiled. Rising back to his feet, he turned to Watson and showed him a curved object on the tip of his finger.

"Is that...a contact lens?" asked Watson in disbelief.

"A glow-in-the-dark one at that," added Sherlock. "There's not much light in here, even in this clearing, it's all night vision for the most part. Perfect place to have something glow."

"Ok, fine. So they're not a pack of wild dogs. They're just...a pack of dogs?"

"Trained dogs, Watson. Trained to kill. Very efficiently if Kenny is anything to go by. The woods are the hunting grounds, and the perfect place to hide a body. Like yours."

"And yours. You're here too."

"Yes, but I wasn't here to start. Baskerville interrogated me in his manor. The moment I was free I came here to find you."

"Grateful. Were you at least tied up? I would hate to think I was the only one who suffered in the last little bit."

Sherlock laughed and shook his head at the notion, "Yes, I was tied up. Thankfully, they didn't search me either, I used my blade kit in my arm to cut my bounds and break free. I called Mycroft, he hopefully will be here soon.

We just have to get out of here before anything else comes our way."

"Agreed, I've had enough of this--"

A growl cut him off, both Sherlock and Watson turned to see the Great Dane from before rising to its feet. Like before, it lowered itself to prepare for its strike. Before either of them could react, a series of barks filled the area, and from the trees next to the Dane came the Belgian Malinois. It broadsided the Dane, forcing it back to the ground.

"It's alive?" said Watson with more disbelief than before.

"Just be glad it's on our side," said Sherlock with a smile. "By the way, I told you so."

The Malinois didn't pay attention to Sherlock or Watson, but focused on the Dane, who was back on its feet. The two dogs growled at one another, each refusing to give an inch to the other. Eventually, they rushed one another, and did their best to strike the other. The Dane had size, but the Malinois had speed and agility, which it used to great effect.

Like a tactical instrument, the Malinois scratched at the Dane's legs, weakening its stance. The Dane fought back, and got a swipe on the Malinois, but that was all it did. With impressive strength, the Malinois head-butted the Dane, knocking it out cold.

Sherlock and Watson were still in awe, this time over the literal dog fight that they had just witnessed. The Malinois finally gazed at them, and walked over to them. Sherlock took the opportunity to bow to the dog, "Thank you again for your help. Watson, thank the dog."

"Uh, thanks. I'm talking to a dog like it's a human. I'm going mad."

"You wish. Now, onto more pressing matters. Do you have any rounds left in your gun?"

Watson reached behind him and pulled out a clip, showing it to Sherlock before loading it into his gun, "This is my last clip. 12 rounds."

"It'll have to do. I'll grab my stick, and between us and the Malinois' help we'll be--"

He stopped as he saw the Malinois look away from them. Its ears perked up, and he focused on the opening to the clearing. Just as quickly as he did though, he beat it out of there, leaving Sherlock and Watson dumbfounded.

"Your "help" just left us, Sherlock," noted Watson with clear annoyance.

"Save the attitude Watson, after all that dog has done for us, I think there's only one reason it would leave like that..."

Sherlock turned to the opening, and from it came Rudolph Baskerville, shotgun in hand. This time though, he wasn't alone, several other people emerged from the opening. Men and woman, all of them armed with guns.

"...it knew it was outmatched."

Baskerville glared at the two of them, but then took a look at the dogs that were scattered throughout the clearing. His face went from anger to rage, "You...you killed my dogs! How many did you kill?!"

"I lost count!" Watson replied challengingly, "You should've told me not to bring a gun to a dog fight!"

"That was a great line, good delivery," praised Sherlock.

Watson smirked at the compliment, but Baskerville continued to fume, "Enjoy your laughs and your jokes. It'll be the last you have."

Unafraid, Watson stepped closer to Baskerville, prompting those around him to point their guns at Watson. This made him stop, but his eyes remained glued to Baskerville, "You want to blame someone for this? Blame yourself! You killed those people, not your dogs, you! Did you really think you would get away with this forever? That no one would figure out your scheme?"

Baskerville slowly cracked a smile, "My scheme? My gosh, you really don't know. Not even you, Mr. Holmes?"

Sherlock grunted, "I wasn't lying when I said I didn't know your motive. I also said I didn't care, and that still remains true."

"You should, you'd be surprised what history can teach you. You think I came up with all this? I didn't. My grandfather did. The war changed him, and it showed him the truth, that the only lives that matter are those loyal to you."

"What kind of crackpot notion is that?" barked Watson.

"The only one that matters. World War II wiped out my family, and what did we get in return? Nothing. Just a missive that the military was grateful for our sacrifice.

Apparently not! But you know who did care? The town. They rallied, they supported my grandfather, and pledged to help him in any way they could. He had no family of his own at the time, so he asked for something to care for. They gave him a dog."

Baskerville smiled, Watson and Sherlock looked at each other nervously.

"My grandfather loved that dog, and he loved the loyalty it gave him, so he got another, and another, until he had his ranch full of dogs. He still felt empty though, he still felt the hatred for the outside world. He wanted payback, no matter how small."

"And that's when the tourists showed up," realized Sherlock.

The smile on Baskerville's face grew wider, and he paced before the two, "Oh yes. Our town had become quite famous. We were untouched by war, that made people curious. So they came, in droves at times, to see what caused us to be untouched. My grandfather was sickened by it, and the townspeople were too. We wanted to be left alone, we wanted to just live our lives in the peace we deserved, that my family died for! But did we get it? No! "

Watson scoffed, he was having none of it, "So your grandfather got mad at tourists and decided to kill them? How noble!"

Angry at the insult on his family, Baskerville went to Watson and hit him in the gut with the butt of his gun, making him fall to his knees. Sherlock tried to help him, but was stopped by the others, who pointed their guns menacingly at him.

"Don't you dare speak of my grandfather that way! He didn't just snap, he saw an opportunity. One of those tourists was a drunk, a bad one. He tried to push himself on one of the townswomen, my grandfather was nearby with some of his dogs when it happened. He saved that girl, and the world lost one drunk."

"A fair trade." mocked Sherlock.

"Mock all you want. It was justice, and it fueled my grandfather, and my father, and now me. Especially when we found out our curse."

"You mean your short life span?"

This statement made Baskerville look at Sherlock intrigued, to which Sherlock smiled back, "Yes, I know about your curse. That offhanded line about your father and grandfather dying around 60, very specific, and very easy to pinpoint why. Your family built this town from the ground up, on their own. Something tells me that cost more than just money.

"Very impressive, Mr. Holmes. The land that my family built Baskerville on was untouched by man outside the battle that happened on it, and in regards to construction before we got to it. So, there was no way of knowing that we built everything on a poisonous material."

"The ground is radioactive?" asked Watson, finally getting back to his feet.

"Not exactly. The mineral is only harmful via direct exposure. Which my family had when they built this place. Everyone else is fine. But the disease is genetic, it's why my family always dies out. Ironically, it's what brought the military to our establishment. They figured it out too. Wanted to test the effects on creatures, including one of my father's dogs."

"Until he burned it down," noted Sherlock. "A random fire? Hardly. Your father likely gave that dog to allay any suspicions. He didn't want that facility there, you don't trust outsiders. So, you let them build it, let them do their work for a while, then when the moment came to strike..."

"He did, and with great pride," Baskerville snickered. "Just like with every death we claim here."

"What did they to you?" shouted Watson, anger returning, "The drunk? Sure, I get that. But not everyone could be that evil. Not all of them deserved to die. Kenny did not deserve to die!"

"Was that the last tourist I fed to my dogs? I don't care to know their names."

Quick as a flash, Watson pointed his gun right at Baskerville's head. The other townspeople pointed theirs at his. Baskerville continued to smile.

"You don't care? Fine. I do."

"Bully for you Mr. Watson. The fact of the matter is, we've done this for years, and the ironic thing? The more killings we did here? The more the people came. The "disappearances" just fueled the attraction that people had with the town. They came, and only some of them left the way they wanted. You think my family brainwashed an entire town? No! They each saw how ignorant and unsympathetic each one of them was. They didn't respect us, we were a tourist attraction. So, we turned it into a tourist trap. A trap that you both are now in."

Watson shook with anger, wanting nothing more than to pull the trigger and end the man's life, even if it meant ending his own.

Sherlock stepped forward, not stopping when some of the guns pointed at him once more, "I was wrong about you, Baskerville."

The surprise returned to Baskerville's face, "Oh?"

"Oh yes, I said before that there was a chance you weren't depraved, I was wrong, you very much are. You want to be left alone? You put up a sign, a warning, a public statement for all to see and hear! You make sure you town isn't a tourist attraction. But you decide to kill the people who visit your town instead? People who wanted nothing more than to see something worth seeing? To possibly solve a mystery? You would deprive them of that, and make their families wonder what really happened to them? You sir are a cad, a foolish man following a crusade of murder by men just as depraved. I will enjoy living so I can testify at your trial about what you did, and what your family did. If it takes me the rest of my life, I will find every victim you killed so that those families can get the closure they deserve. Then, I will make sure your little town of horrors rots for its compliance in these acts. Do you hear me, Baskerville!?"

Sherlock breathed heavily after his statement. Watson looked at Sherlock in shock, he had rarely seen him this infuriated at a person, and never for such an emotional reason.

Baskerville just gazed at Sherlock, his expression stone-faced, "Are you done?"

"Yes."

"Good."

He raised his shotgun at Sherlock's head, who didn't even flinch at the action. A large rustling noise caught all of their ears though, and from all around them, silhouettes appeared.

"Freeze! Nobody move!"

As these silhouettes drew closer, it became clear that they were soldiers, fully decked out in combat gear and machine guns. Each of which were pointed at Baskerville and the townsfolk. Watson laughed in relief at the turn of events, while Sherlock just smiled and looked around for something.

"Glad I made it in time," came a smug voice.

Sherlock and Watson turned to see Mycroft emerging from the trees and into the clearing. Though his expression was as smug as his voice, Watson could see similar relief on his face at seeing them both alive and mostly unharmed.

"You're late, brother," teased Sherlock, still smiling.

"Hardly. You said I had an hour, I made it to this spot in exactly fifty-seven minutes and forty-four seconds. See?"

He pulled out his phone and showed them a stop watch which was paused on exactly that number.

Watson broke out into laughter again, "You two are something else."

"That we are, Watson. In truth, you're lucky I made it here at all. I had to summon these men and get a ride, and all without much of an explanation as to why."

Sherlock rolled his eyes, "Right, because saving lives and stopping a town wide conspiracy isn't reason enough."

"Not for some brother," noted Mycroft, who then gave a kind smile. "But it is for me, especially when one of those lives is my family."

A loud scoff got their attention, they turned to see Baskerville glaring at them, "You can take your sentiment and choke on it. You think this is over because I'm arrested? The town will hear of this and-"

Before he could finish, Mycroft pulled out a gun and pointed it right at his forehead, not unlike what Watson did earlier. However, Mycroft wasn't shaking, his resolve was true.

"Sir, you would be wise to silence yourself. You tried to kill my brother, and his friend, and have killed many more. And as for your "town", I have reinforcements on the way. You'll find that life is about to be very different in Baskerville. Or rather, you'll hear about it via letters from your prison cell. Take them away."

The soldiers nodded in acknowledgement, then began to lead them out of the clear and into the dark of the forest.

Once gone, Sherlock turned back to his brother, "There could still be wild dogs out there."

Mycroft smirked, "I heard your warning, brother. Each of them have a device that'll emit a frequency that repels dogs. Military grade in fact. They'll be fine, as will we. On that note, we should leave, if for no other reason than Watson here needs some medical attention. I have some medical personnel coming in the first wave of reinforcements. We'll get your stitched up right, Watson."

Watson gave a small bow, "I appreciate that, Mycroft. Truly, I hurt all over."

"Then let us get going," suggested Sherlock, "This forest and its inhabitants have taken enough."

With a nod from each of them, they made their way out. Sherlock supported Watson as they left.

Chapter Seven: What Are We Allowed To Feel?

The next few days were a blur for Sherlock and Watson. Mycroft's reinforcements arrived, and immediately stormed the town to ensure no incidents occurred while Rudolph Baskerville was taken away. When asked what would honestly happen to the town, Mycroft merely said that an investigation would take place over the next few months to see who was a willing collaborator, and who just stood by and let it happen. Those who confessed or were caught with evidence would be arrested, the rest would be allowed to remain.

This didn't sit well with either Sherlock or Watson, but they knew that because of the way the killings were done, it would be impossible to try them all for it. So the next best thing was to make sure it never happened again, to which Mycroft noted that the town would be under constant surveillance to ensure that it didn't.

Watson got patched up by some doctors. His wounds were more severe than he realized, but because he got treated, he would only need a few days bed rest once he returned to London. Though Mycroft suggested checking in with a proper hospital when he had the chance.

While Watson was being treated, Sherlock returned to the forest, where he was greeted by the Belgian Malinois. With the dogs' help, he found the body of Kenny, and put it in a body bag for transport back to his sister.

The remaining dogs from Baskerville's pack were rounded up by the soldiers. Some decided to fight, and were put down because of it. A few ran, and when they exited the forest, they became entirely different dogs entirely. They were not only not aggressive, but playful, and tried to play with the soldiers when they emerged from the forest.

Watson saw this and was flabbergasted, "What was that?"

"Conditioning, Watson," revealed Sherlock. "Remember, the dogs were all over town. At night, they likely went back to the ranch, or the forest. Baskerville, and those who helped him, likely trained the dogs to attack anyone they met in the forest. With a few exceptions of course. When they're outside the forest, they're perfect playful pups. Inside the forest?"

"Demon dogs."

"For lack of a better term, yes. It's not unlike a doctor going into a zone once a surgery has started."

"Or a detective tuning out everything else to understand a clue."

Watson smiled at Sherlock, who shook his head at the jest, "Well played, but yes. Same principal. I'll make sure to remind Mycroft to make this place a "No Dog

Zone" for the next few years. And to make the forest off limits to anyone, just in case a few dogs remain."

"Is it wrong for me to say that I'd rather just burn the forest down?" asked Watson with an odd tone and a mixed expression.

"Wrong? No. Out of character? A bit. But under the circumstances, I do understand your feelings on this. Environmentalists won't though."

This time Sherlock smiled at Watson, who couldn't stifle a laugh, "Shut up, Sherlock."

"Come on, let's go help Mycroft settle some things. Then we need to return home. We have some things to take care of ourselves."

Their remaining time in the town of Baskerville was used to help set things up for the future, as well as get their things before leaving. Mycroft offered to fly them home, but the two declined, deciding to take the train back. They wanted the time and quiet to contemplate what had happened to them.

On the train, Sherlock and Watson sat quietly for much of the trip. Only after an odd thought came into Watson's mind did he turn to his friend, "Sherlock? That monologue you gave to Baskerville, did you know the soldiers were around us when you said that?"

Sherlock gave a small smile, and an equally small shake of the head, "No. I felt compelled to say it. I knew it might be the last thing I said, but it felt right at the time. I had no knowledge of my brother being so close. For once, I wasn't paying attention to anything but what was right in front of me."

"I've never heard you be that passionate before. Kind, sure, irritated, of course. But that? That was different, different for you. Where did that come from?"

"I guess it has to do with that Belgian Malinois."

"What? What does the dog have to do with anything?"

"Because it reminded me that I wanted a dog when I was a child."

This reveal took Watson aback, Sherlock had never openly talked about his childhood before, "Really?"

He nodded, "Oh yes, I wanted one quite badly when I was a child."

"Why didn't you get it?"

"Parents wouldn't allow it."

"What? Why not?"

Sherlock looked away and out the train window, his expression went to one of pure sadness, another thing that Watson rarely saw from his friend.

"You don't have to tell me if you don't want to, Sherlock."

"Hmm? Oh, no, I was just thinking about it all. To answer your question, I would like you to recall what I said my parents in our previous conversation of my past."

"They were...protective?"

"Yes, but it wouldn't be a lie to say they weren't protective of me and Mycroft, but rather, of our brains, our intelligence."

"I don't follow," noted Watson with a confused shake of the head.

Sherlock shifted in place, an uncomfortable look growing on his face, "My parents did well enough in life, yet both of them had a complex that made them regret not doing more. When they had Mycroft and myself, they swore that both of us would become something greater than they were. Better. More distinguished, more respected."

"Ah, I see where this is going."

"Maybe. I told you how my parents handpicked our curriculum, that was true, but it was designed with an intent to guide us on a path that led to their own goals, not ours. To ensure that we were focused on those goals, they didn't let us do certain things. No friends, very little television, and no pets."

Watson again shook his head, but this time out of sadness for Sherlock, "I can't imagine."

"Good," Sherlock replied with a laugh. "Anyway, one day, when I was around ten, I thought I had the perfect plan to get them to let me have a dog. I researched every breed out there to try and find one that I felt would match our family to a tee. I studied their histories, their builds, breeding habits, all of it. I ended up...on a Belgian Malinois."

"You're kidding."

"I am not. They're good dogs, they were raised for herding at one time, are incredibly intelligent, yet require patience from the owner if they're to be pets. I compiled all the research I did on the dog, requested an audience with my parents, and laid it all out for them."

"Bet that went over well."

Sherlock hesitated, his expression went blank, and only after some deep breaths did he return his gaze to Watson, "They...beat me."

Watson couldn't believe it, "What? Because you asked for a dog?"

"They said, "Your dreams and curiosities should be focused on what we tell you to be." They were furious that instead of my studies that I decided to research this. So my father took me to another room and punished me with a cane."

Watson couldn't help but gap at this, the idea of such a major punishment for something that wasn't even close to a crime, and from a parent no less, was unfathomable to him.

He tried to form comforting words, but none came, "I don't know what to say, Sherlock."

Sherlock shrugged nonchalantly, "There's nothing to say, nor could anything you say change anything. Ironically, after that...incident, I started to become what I am today."

"An arrogant, mystery-addicted, know-it-all?"

Watson smiled as Sherlock looked at him, and they both shared a much needed laugh, "Thank you for knowing exactly how to describe me, Watson."

"It's my honor," Watson replied with an over-the-top voice and a bow of the head.

"What I meant was, after that, I knew I didn't want to be what my parents wanted me to be. But I also didn't want to get beaten again, so I played by their rules when they were looking, and played by my own when they weren't. It's funny, I think that's where my love of mysteries started to shine through. I started to ask questions about why my parents were so forceful in regards to what path I took. I looked for mysteries where I could find them. Tested myself to enhance my observation skills, knowledge absorption, anything I thought was necessary. I was so determined that by the time I reached college..."

A look of revelation came upon Watson's face, "...you were bursting to test it all. Away from them. Dear gosh, no wonder you were insufferable."

"No doubt, and I still am today despite your best efforts," teased Sherlock.

"You're not dead yet, I'll make a gentleman out of you eventually."

"I'd take a bet on that."

The two smiled, then went silent again. The countryside continued to pass by. Watson watched it for a while, but his gaze kept going back to Sherlock.

"Sherlock?"

"Hmm?"

"What did your parents want you to be?"

A low laugh came from Sherlock as he thought about it, "A professor."

"Of what?" asked Watson in disbelief.

"Anything substantial. They were partial to math or science, but I choose a path that I felt could trick them into letting me do what I want.'

"Language. That's why you did it."

"I convinced them that if I learned language along with certain other studies that I could teach abroad at all the wondrous institutions that the world had to offer. Whereas in truth, I was just adding to my skills to ensure I could take on as many cases as possible. The language aspect has been very helpful though, I won't lie."

"Oh yes, I remember that Russian case, that would've be difficult without you being multilingual."

"Spasiba."

"Your parents do know what you do now, right?"

This time, an evil smile appeared on Sherlock's face, this slightly unnerved Watson, but Sherlock didn't care this time, "Oh yes, they know. Didn't you know that our school loans are massively different in quantities? My parents paid for my entire ride the first time. Then, when you went to medical school and I took extra courses they got suspicious. So I came clean. I've been cutoff ever since, and I was so happy when they did."

"Really?"

"Yes, the money was their last bit of control over me. Without it I was forced to fend for myself. I could finally be myself without ties, without restrictions, without fear of what they would do to me. That's why I reacted like I did with Baskerville. As much as I detest what people do at times, I would never restrict them from trying something they want to do. I can tell when they'll fail, but it's better to fail and learn than never to try at all. The question that I can't help but ask when thinking about them is, "What are we allowed to feel?" There's nothing wrong with curiosity, and there's nothing disrespectful about it either. Having your own desires, your own dreams, the urge to do something even if you feel motivated or compelled to not do it. There's nothing wrong with that. Baskerville didn't understand that. My parents didn't understand that. I bet they would've gotten along actually."

"That's a bit harsh," stated Watson.

"So were they. I told you the worst thing did to me, Watson, but there are plenty of other things they did that were bad too. I don't insult them lightly."

"Fair enough. One last question, if I may."

"You may," answered Sherlock, a curious expression now growing, "but I'm holding you to that remark."

"I have no doubt. Your parents wanted you to be a professor, what did they want Mycroft to be?"

A more jovial laugh emanated from Sherlock this time, which made even Watson smile upon hearing it. Once Sherlock quieted down he addressed the question, "Ironically, they did feel government work would suit him best. Just not in the way he's in now. Naturally, they're proud that he serves his country like he does. The perfect son."

"With respect, neither of you are anywhere close to perfect."

"And I'm more than happy to admit that."

With a final smile to the other, they again went quite and observed the view from the outside world. With each passing minute they drew closer to London, where they would be safe and sound. Even if only for a little while.

Epilogue: Of Dogs And Men

London. A home to many, including Watson and Sherlock. As they disembarked the train onto the busy station, they couldn't help but take notice of the larger crowds they found themselves in. For while Baskerville had a big enough populace, it was nothing compared to London.

Luggage in hand, they made their way through London Waterloo Station. Passing through crowds of people as they did. The two looked at the people with cautious eyes, but few looked back. If they did, it was out of curiosity for why they were being looked at, or because they had accidentally bumped into them and they looked to them to apologize.

The feeling of not being hunted took a bit to get over, especially for Watson, who repeatedly looked at and touched his bandages from where the dogs had hurt him. For Sherlock, it was merely the fact that the whole the people around him weren't out to get him that took a while to get over. He had been suspicious of the people of Baskerville from the moment he arrived more or less, and it persisted until they were on the train home. Now that he was back, he found it hard to turn off the need to be alert of all who were around him.

Feelings in check, they made their way to the street, and hailed a taxi. The two didn't talk while they were driven home, nor when they arrived back at 221B Baker St. Mrs. Hudson greeted them, and they exchanged some pleasantries with her, but she could tell that they wanted to rest from their ordeal. So she let them go up to their room.

Finally back in their apartment, they made for their rooms and started to unpack their things. Watson unlocked his suitcase and smiled as he noticed all his clothing and items were still perfect in their placement.

"Still got it," he murmured to himself.

With a small smile he began to unpack everything. As he lowered himself to put some of his attire in the nearby dresser he winced in pain. The wounds were still fresh, and while the bandages helped keep him together, they weren't fixes for the pain. Toughing it out, Watson was able to put all his things away.

Once done he put his hands in his pockets and sighed. As he did, his phone went off, and he pulled it out. After he turned it on he saw a text message from Mary reading, "Let me know when you are home."

Another sigh followed, and Watson looked away from the message with an expression of uncertainty. Yet again though, he toughed up, and hit a button to call her. He sat down as the phone rang.

Eventually, he heard Mary's voice and smiled, "Hey Mary. I'm back. ...yeah, case is done. No... not a lot went right."

In the living room, Sherlock sat in his chair and just pondered. This was one of the few times he let his mind drift, and because of that, his thoughts went from the case, to Watson, to his parents, Mycroft, the Belgian Malinois, and more. If a thought pattern became too painful he shunted his head in a direction as if to throw the thought out of his mind, and moved on to the next one. Frustration built though as he couldn't find something peaceful to think about. He only snapped out of his funk when Watson's voiced entered the room.

"No Mary. No, Mary! Do not come over!" shouted Watson, now fully in the room and looking exasperated, "Because I'm not going to be here that long. We have some things to take care of, then I'm heading to the hospital to check out my wounds. If you want to see me, I'll text you when I'm my way to the hospital. I am not being difficult! You're the one over exaggerating things!"

This went on for a little bit, Sherlock found joy in their relationship woes, and soon was smiling and laughing at their argument.

Watson though was having no such feelings, as Mary continued to try and push her will on him, "I'll...I'll contact....I'll contact you on the way to the hospital! Goodbye!"

He ended the call, and tossed his phone onto the nearby chair. An angry sigh followed, along with a glare to Sherlock, who was still smiling.

"Not. A. Word."

"Of course not," teased Sherlock with a grin, "you don't need my help to be more miserable right now."

"You don't--"

He was cut off when his phone began to ring. Watson slowly moved towards it to see who was calling, it was Mary. With a groan he shook his head and walked away.

"Why must she get so worked up like this? I thought she would be happy I was being honest with her about what happened!"

"While I may not be enlightened on relationships, I do know that women are complicated creatures," mused Sherlock.

"You don't need a degree or a detective mind to know that, Sherlock."

"True, but it still needs to be said."

"Fair enough. So, you holding up?"

Sherlock shrugged, "I'll be fine. It's you who should be asked that question. You really going to the hospital?"

Watson nodded, "Yeah. Mycroft brought in some good doctors, but I'm going to need some pain meds for at least a week while this heals. Don't worry, I won't get addicted."

"I would make sure you don't."

"Oh, I have no doubt of that. But I felt that needed to be said. Regardless, we do have one last job before this case is over."

Sherlock rose from his chair, and nodded. Watson went and grabbed both his phone and his jacket, and the two proceeded out the door.

A little while away, they soon found themselves in the house of Dee, the sister of Kenny. She welcomed them into her home, and once inside, they explained the events of what happened to both her brother, to them, and to the town. Both offered to give an abridged version, but she wanted to hear it all. So they gave it to her.

Sherlock and Watson took turns telling the story, until finally they were done.

"Your brothers' body will arrive within the next day or so," noted Sherlock, "We asked our friend Mia Harper to contact you when it arrives. He'll be waiting for you at the city morgue."

"I appreciate that," replied Dee with a small smile, "I was sure I was never going to see him again. At least now I can say goodbye."

"Your whole family can," added Watson.

"Right, right."

She laughed lightly, and rose from her spot so that she could walk around. This got the attention of both of them.

"Are you alright?" asked Sherlock

"I don't think anyone in this room is alright, Mr. Holmes," she answered politely.

"You're very right, but what's on your mind?"

"I just don't understand how a whole town could do this. A person? Sure. A group? Yeah, probably. But hundreds of people? If not more? All of them willing to do this? It doesn't make sense."

Watson sympathized with her confusion, and tried to comfort her with a smile, "If you had told me when you came to us that we would be fighting a town full of trained dogs that attacked tourists, we wouldn't have believed you. Not even him."

"I might have believed the town part, but not the dogs," joked Sherlock, but he grew serious right after. "Hate is something that grows. It starts simple, but then it multiplies, amplifies. It's something that can be buried until the absolutely right moment. And then? When it unleashes? It's terrible. The town of Baskerville had a lot of hate. They felt slighted, wronged by those who would impose on their quiet life. So they bided their time and lashed out. It's not an excuse, it's just what happened."

Dee seemed to find solace in this, but something was nagging at her, "Why Kenny though? Why him and not me? Or why not both of us?"

"I think you already know the answer," stated Watson sadly. "When you came to us, you said that Kenny wanted to go explore some landmark in the town. Am I right to guess that was the only time you were separated?"

"Yes...yes it was."

Sherlock stepped forward, "These people were opportunists, Dee. They used this to lure people to where they needed them to be. Not unlike how we got flash-banged by the cops. Rudolph Baskerville probably thought we would go to his mansion after we saw the town empty, so he made sure his men were waiting for us. For Kenny, they were simply waiting for an opening to grab one of you."

"So it could've been me?" she asked with a sad smile.

"Yes."

"Sherlock," chastised Watson.

"Lying would do her no good, Watson. It could've been her. Or, just as likely, if they felt you two wouldn't separate, they could've taken you both."

Dee gave her odd laugh again, "Scary thought. Both of us killed by those dogs."

"But you weren't. You made it out. You found us. We found Kenny, and then we found out what the town was doing. We know that doesn't bring Kenny back, but it does mean something. Do you know what?"

"...it wasn't in vain."

"Or meaningless. Families from all over are going to get the news that we're giving you now. And they'll get closure of a sort. Maybe not what they want, but they'll get it."

"I suppose that's all we can ask for, given all of this."

The three went silent. Dee just looked at her feet, while Watson and Sherlock focused on her, waiting to see if there was anything else she needed from them.

After a bit, she smiled, and nodded before bowing to them, "I am in your debt Mr. Holmes, Mr. Watson. I won't forget this."

The two bowed their heads to her in reply, Sherlock straightened himself up first, "It was our honor."

Watson smiled kindly at her, "And our pleasure. If you need anything from us, just let us know."

She promised that she would, and then guided them out of the house. Now finished, Watson hailed a cab to go to the hospital. Sherlock said he would walk home. Watson laughed, as the trek would be several miles, but he didn't argue and got in the cab.

Hours later, both were at 221B Baker St., Watson was relaxing in his chair, new bandages on him and painkillers in him. He listened to Sherlock, who was playing his violin.

The tune he played was very symphonic in nature. It started out slow, weaving heavy on long notes to bring true emphasis to the sound. As he went on, the pace picked up, as if to build up intrigue. Then, the speed increased rapidly, filling the room with a sound of danger and that of a chase.

Sherlock then mixed the paces to create something uneven, yet perfectly balanced within the story and song he was playing. Finally, he danced the bow just a little bit more, and slowly closed out the piece.

Done with the song, Sherlock lowered his violin and looked out the window he was facing. Watson smiled and clapped, "That was very lively."

"Thank you, Watson," replied Sherlock, not facing him just yet.

"I could tell you were trying to mimic our case, was that fast part me getting chased by the dogs?"

"Yes. Too much?"

"No, no, just right. It was all very well done."

Sherlock couldn't help but smile at this, and soon moved towards his violin case near his chair. As he put it away, he eyed Watson, "Medication kicking in?"

"Oh yes, I feel good right now. Only took twice the recommended dosage."

"That's not funny, Watson."

"Sorry, sorry, the drugs do have me a little loopy. I'm taking the prescribed amount, I promise."

Content, Sherlock nodded, "Good, I don't want you to go through what I did."

A small, sad smile grew on Watson's face, "I know, and as a doctor I would be ashamed if I let that happen to me. I'll lighten up on the jokes."

"Appreciated. So, once you're fully healed, are you going to write this up?"

This time Watson laughed, "Honestly? I'm not sure. It's like Dee said, it's hard to believe. Not that some of our cases aren't had to believe anyway, but this? This is another league."

Sherlock sat down in his chair and pondered the truth behind this, "True. A decades long grudge against outsiders, dogs that are feral in a forest but perfectly tame outside it, it is the stuff legends are made out of. You might be better off not writing it. Although, if you do, I have the perfect name this time."

"Oh?"

"The Hounds Of Baskerville."

He paused, and waited for Watson's answer. Watson thought over it for a bit and nodded, smiling widely as he thought about it more, "That is pretty good, Sherlock. You finally got a good title."

"Ha! Ironic though, the one I get is the one you might not write."

"We'll see how it goes. However, you did forget to mention something in that recap of our case."

"Oh? What's that?" asked Sherlock curious.

Watson gaped at the question, "What's that? The Belgian Malinois! That dog was not normal even by Baskerville standards. That dog was intelligent, far more intelligent than it should've been. How do you explain that?"

A low laughter came from Sherlock, and he again turned to the window, and looked outside it. He smiled as he thought of certain things, "Watson, I am a man of certain beliefs. Would you agree?"

"I would."

"Those beliefs have been earned through years of study and encounters. I believe in both coincidence and cosmic intervention, on a certain scale of course. I believe in good and evil, right and wrong. I believe in both science and magic...to an extent. I've seen many things, and in regards to the Belgian Malinois, I am reminded of a phrase I told a professor once when he tried to stump me with an "impossible" question."

Intrigued, Watson leaned in, "Which is?"

"When you have eliminated the impossible, whatever remains, however improbable, must be the truth."

"Very interesting. But what does it mean in our case?"

"Well, the Belgian Malinois is clearly not a normal dog, right?"

"Right."

"Exactly. So, the only possible, and probable, conclusion we have left is that something made it not normal. Genetics? Evolution? Something in the forest? Who can say? All we know, and all we need to know, is that something did happen to that dog, and because of it, it's as smart as a human, if not smarter. That's enough for me."

Sherlock smiled widely at Watson, who rolled his eyes and got up, "I hate you."

"I know."

Happy with the acknowledgement, Watson went down the hallway and then entered his room, closing the door behind him as he did. Sherlock remained in the living room, but rose up to head to the window once again. He looked up to the sky, seeing the stars as they shined brightly down.

Far away, near Baskerville, the Belgian Malinois looked up at the stars as well. The dog had a very curious look in its eye. A longing of sorts. Eventually, the dog lowered its gaze and headed back into the forest.

It walked on a path for a long time, then went through some brush and trees until eventually it ended up in a protected area where a little dog house of sorts stood. It was made of tree branches and covered in leaves, moss, and vines to ensure that heat was trapped inside the house.

The dog seemed to smile as it looked at its home, then ran right into the opening and moved around a little to get comfortable. As the dog lowered itself to the ground, its tailed swished back and forth. When it did, the tail caught something nearby and flung it. The Malinois noticed this, and went over to pick it up in its mouth.

It brought it back to the doghouse and laid it right in front, then proceeded to lay back down in his house.

The item the dog retrieved was a very old dog collar. Right in the center was a dog tag, and on it, was the name, "Fido."

www.ingramcontent.com/pod-product-compliance
Lightning Source LLC
Chambersburg PA
CBHW071906220626
47052CB00002B/235